The Concepts of a Plan

Aaron Abilene

Published by Syphon Creative, 2024.

THE CONCEPTS OF A PLAN

First edition. November 4, 2024.

ISBN: 979-8227276100

Written by Aaron Abilene.

Also by Aaron Abilene

505
505
505: Resurrection

Balls
Dead Awake
Before The Dead Awake
Dead Sleep
Bulletproof Balls

Carnival Game
Full Moon Howl
Donovan
Shades of Z

Codename
The Man in The Mini Van

Deadeye
Deadeye & Friends
Cowboys Vs Aliens

Ferris
Life in Prescott
Afterlife in Love
Tragic Heart

Island
Paradise Island
The Lost Island
The Lost Island 2
The Lost Island 3
The Island 2

Pandemic
Pandemic

Prototype
Prototype
The Compound

Slacker
Slacker 2
Slacker 3
Slacker: Dead Man Walkin'

Survivor Files
Survivor Files: Day 1
Survivor Files : Day 1 Part 2
Survivor Files : Day 2
Survivor Files : On The Run
Survivor Files : Day 3
Survivor Files : Day 4
Survivor Files : Day 5
Survivor Files : Day 6
Survivor Files : Day 7
Survivor Files : Day 8
Survivor Files : Day 9
Survivor Files : Day 10
Survivor Files : Day 11
Survivor Files : Day 12
Survivor Files : Day 13
Survivor Files : Day 14
Survivor Files : Day 15
Survivor Files : Day 16
Survivor Files : Day 17
Survivor Files : Day 18

Texas

Devil Child of Texas
A Vampire in Texas

The Author
Breaking Wind
Yellow Snow
Dragon Snatch
Golden Showers
Nether Region
Evil Empire

Thomas
Quarantine
Contagion
Eradication
Isolation
Immune
Pathogen
Bloodline
Decontaminated

TPD
Trailer Park Diaries
Trailer Park Diaries 2
Trailer Park Diaries 3

Virus
Raising Hell

Zombie Bride
Zombie Bride
Zombie Bride 2
Zombie Bride 3

Standalone
The Victims of Pinocchio
A Christmas Nightmare
Pain
Fat Jesus
A Zombie's Revenge
The Headhunter
Crash
Tranq
The Island
Dog
The Quiet Man
Joe Superhero
Feral
Good Guys
Romeo and Juliet and Zombies
The Gamer
Becoming Alpha
Dead West
Small Town Blues

Shades of Z: Redux
The Gift of Death
Killer Claus
Skarred
Home Sweet Home
Alligator Allan
10 Days
Army of The Dumbest Dead
Kid
The Cult of Stupid
9 Time Felon
Slater
Bad Review: Hannah Dies
Me Again
Maurice and Me
The Family Business
Lightning Rider : Better Days
Lazy Boyz
The Sheep
Wild
The Flood
Extinction
Good Intentions
Dark Magic
Sparkles The Vampire Clown
From The Future, Stuck in The Past
Rescue
Knock Knock
Creep
Honest John
Urbex
She's Psycho
Unfinished

Neighbors
Misery, Nevada
Vicious Cycle
Relive
Romeo and Juliet: True Love Conquers All
Dead Road
Florida Man
Hunting Sarah
The Great American Zombie Novel
Carnage
Marge 3 Toes
Random Acts of Stupidity
Born Killer
The Abducted
Whiteboy
Broken Man
Graham Hiney
Bridge
15
Paper Soldiers
Zartan
The Concepts of a Plan
The Firsts in Life
Giant Baby

The Concepts of a Plan

Written by Aaron Abilene

Daniel shuffled forward in the seemingly endless grocery store line, a hefty stack of crumpled forms and dog-eared paperwork clutched to his chest. The fluorescent lights buzzed overhead, casting a sickly pallor on the faces of the bedraggled shoppers. He glanced at his watch and groaned. Two hours. Two goddamn hours he'd been standing here, and he was still a dozen people from the counter.

A bead of sweat trickled down his temple as he eyed the confounding array of forms splayed out before him on a rickety card table. Form 27B-6... or was it 62B-7? Christ, it was like trying to decipher hieroglyphics. He snatched one from the pile, squinting at the microscopic print.

"Attention, shoppers," a nasally voice droned over the crackling intercom. "Remember, blue forms must be filled out in triplicate, and red forms require a blood sample and retinal scan. Have your genetically encoded ID card ready, or you will be sent to the back of the line. Again."

"You gotta be shittin' me," Daniel muttered. He patted his pockets, trying to recall where he stashed his ID card. Probably wedged between the couch cushions back at his flop. Perfect.

The line inched forward at a glacial pace. Daniel could feel his sanity slipping away with each passing minute. He'd already missed half a day's work, and his measly pay would barely cover a week's worth of tasteless government-issued rations.

Finally, he reached the counter, slamming his crumpled stack of paperwork in front of a sourpuss of a government drone, her beady eyes sizing him up like a stale hunk of bread.

1

"I need a pint of milk and a box of cereal. Here's my ration card," Daniel said, mustering what little politeness remained in his sleep-deprived body.

The clerk curled her lip in disgust. "Form 82C is missing a signature. Back of the line."

"Are you kidding? I've been here for two goddamn hours!" Daniel's patience snapped like a frayed rubber band.

The clerk remained unmoved, her expression as vacant as a department store mannequin's. "Rules are rules. No exceptions."

Daniel leaned over the counter, a simmering rage boiling just beneath his skin. He locked eyes with the bureaucratic banshee, ready to unleash a verbal onslaught that would make a sailor blush.

Daniel's gaze wandered down the winding line, a sea of wearied faces and slumped shoulders, when he spotted two familiar figures. Alice and Kyle, his partners in dystopian misery, were a dozen spots behind, their arms weighed down by precarious stacks of paperwork.

"Well, if it isn't Tweedledee and Tweedledum," Daniel muttered under his breath, a wry grin tugging at the corners of his mouth.

He watched as Alice fumbled with her forms, a cascade of white sheets fluttering to the grimy linoleum. Kyle, ever the gentleman, bent down to help, only to have his own stack topple like a Jenga tower.

"Smooth move, Ex-Lax," Daniel called out, his voice cutting through the drone of the fluorescent lights.

Alice's head snapped up, her eyes narrowing as she spotted Daniel. "Well, if it isn't Mr. Sunshine himself. What's the matter, Danny Boy? Paperwork got your panties in a twist?"

"Nah, just enjoying the five-star service," Daniel retorted, gesturing to the line that seemed to stretch to the horizon. "I'm thinking of setting up a tent and roasting marshmallows. Care to join?"

Kyle chuckled, shaking his head. "I'd rather eat my own shoe than spend another minute in this hellhole."

"Hey, don't knock it 'til you've tried it," Alice quipped, a mischievous glint in her eye. "I hear the leather is quite tender this time of year."

Daniel couldn't help but crack a smile. Leave it to these two to find humor in the most soul-crushing of situations. He glanced back at the clerk, who was watching the exchange with a disapproving scowl.

"Better get back in line," Daniel sighed, gathering his paperwork. "Wouldn't want to keep the Wicked Witch waiting."

As he trudged to the back of the queue, Daniel's mind churned with frustration. There had to be a way to outsmart this ridiculous system, to beat the bureaucrats at their own game. He just needed a plan, a stroke of genius that would leave them all slack-jawed and stuttering.

Thoughts raced through Daniel's mind as he pondered his next move. He couldn't afford to waste any more time in this godforsaken line, but he also couldn't risk getting on the wrong side of the government goons. He needed to be smart, to find a loophole in their twisted rules and regulations.

Alice and Kyle's banter faded into the background as Daniel retreated into his own head, his brow furrowed in concentration. There had to be a way, a chink in the armor of this dystopian nightmare. And he was going to find it, even if it meant risking everything he had left.

With a sudden burst of inspiration, Daniel's eyes lit up, a mischievous grin spreading across his face. He glanced down at the stack of paperwork in his hands, the gears in his mind turning as a plan began to take shape. It was a long shot, but if it worked, he'd be hailed as a hero by the downtrodden masses.

"Alright, here goes nothing," Daniel muttered under his breath, straightening his shoulders and marching towards the front of the line with a newfound sense of purpose.

As he approached the counter, Daniel slapped his paperwork down with a resounding thud, startling the clerk out of her bureaucratic stupor. She glared at him, her eyes narrowing with suspicion.

"Excuse me, sir, but you can't just-"

"Can't what?" Daniel interrupted, his voice dripping with false sincerity. "Can't follow the rules? Can't play by the book? Well, I've got news for you, sweetheart. I've done my homework."

He tapped the stack of papers with a finger, his grin widening. "You see, according to Article 42, Subsection B of the Grocery Acquisition Guidelines, any citizen who presents a fully completed Form 1138-X is entitled to immediate service, regardless of their position in line."

The clerk's mouth opened and closed like a fish out of water, her eyes darting between Daniel and the paperwork. "But... but that form doesn't exist!" she sputtered.

"Oh, but it does," Daniel replied smoothly, sliding a sheet of paper from the middle of the stack. "I have it right here, signed and notarized by the Director of Grocery Affairs himself."

He watched with barely contained glee as the clerk's face turned a sickly shade of green, her hands shaking as she reached for the form. It was a thing of beauty, a masterpiece of forgery that would have made even the most seasoned con artist proud.

As the clerk studied the document, Daniel's heart pounded in his chest, the thrill of the con coursing through his veins. This was the moment of truth, the point of no return. If she bought it, he'd be home free. If not... well, he didn't want to think about that.

The clerk squinted at the form, her brow furrowed in concentration. Daniel held his breath, his palms sweating as he waited for her verdict. Finally, after what felt like an eternity, she let out a defeated sigh.

"Everything appears to be in order," she grumbled, handing the form back to Daniel. "I'll process your purchase right away, sir."

Daniel flashed her a winning smile, his eyes twinkling with mischief. "Thank you so much for your assistance," he said, laying the charm on thick. "I knew I could count on a dedicated public servant like yourself to uphold the integrity of our great bureaucratic system."

The clerk merely grunted in response, her fingers flying over the keys of her ancient computer terminal. Daniel's gaze wandered to the line behind him, where Alice and Kyle stood, their mouths agape in amazement. He shot them a sly wink, reveling in the thrill of his victory.

As the clerk handed him his receipt and a handful of ration coupons, Daniel couldn't help but feel a surge of pride. He had done it, beaten the system at its own game. Sure, it was a small victory in the grand scheme of things, but in a world where every day was a struggle, he'd take what he could get.

"Have a pleasant day, sir," the clerk muttered, her voice dripping with sarcasm.

"Oh, I will," Daniel replied, shoving his paperwork back into his bag. "And remember, the next time someone tries to pull a fast one on you, just ask yourself: What would Daniel do?"

With that, he turned on his heel and strutted away from the counter, his head held high. He could feel the eyes of the other shoppers on him, their envy and admiration palpable in the air. Let them stare, he thought. Let them see what a true master of the game looked like.

As Daniel basked in the glory of his triumph, Alice and Kyle rushed to the counter, their arms laden with crumpled forms and faded receipts. They fumbled with their paperwork, their frustration mounting as they tried to make sense of the byzantine rules and regulations.

"Form 27B-6?" the clerk droned, her voice as flat as her affect. "I'm sorry, but you'll need to fill out Form 82C-9 first, then take it to the Department of Redundancy Department for approval."

Alice let out a groan, her eyes rolling back in her head. "You've got to be kidding me," she muttered, snatching the form from the clerk's hand. "This is the third time I've been sent to that damn department today."

Kyle, meanwhile, was engaged in a heated argument with another clerk, his face turning a delightful shade of purple. "What do you mean, my ration card is expired?" he sputtered, waving the tattered piece of paper in the air. "I just got it last week!"

Daniel watched the chaos unfold, a smirk playing at the corners of his mouth. He knew he should probably offer to help his friends, but where was the fun in that? Besides, they needed to learn to fend for themselves in this messed-up world.

Just as he was about to turn away, Alice caught his eye, her gaze pleading. "Daniel," she called out, her voice tinged with desperation. "Can you give us a hand here? We're drowning in paperwork."

Daniel hesitated for a moment, weighing his options. On the one hand, he had already completed his own grocery run and was eager to get home and enjoy his hard-earned spoils. On the other hand, he couldn't just leave his friends to fend for themselves. With a sigh, he strode back to the counter, his swagger never faltering.

"Step aside, amateurs," he declared, elbowing Kyle out of the way. "Let me show you how it's done."

With a flourish, Daniel snatched the paperwork from Alice's hands and began filling it out at lightning speed, his pen flying across the page. He muttered under his breath as he worked, his brow furrowed in concentration.

"Form 82C-9, my ass," he grumbled, scribbling furiously. "More like Form 82C-waste-of-my-damn-time."

Alice and Kyle watched in awe as Daniel navigated the bureaucratic labyrinth with ease, his confidence never wavering. Within minutes, he had completed all the necessary forms and presented them to the clerk with a flourish.

"There," he said, dusting off his hands. "That should do it. Now, can we please get our damn groceries and get out of here?"

The clerk scanned the paperwork, her eyes widening in surprise. "Well, well, well," she murmured, a hint of admiration in her voice. "It seems everything is in order. Congratulations, you three. You've successfully completed your grocery shopping."

Alice and Kyle let out a whoop of joy, high-fiving each other in celebration. Daniel, for his part, simply shrugged, a satisfied smirk on his face.

"All in a day's work," he said, grabbing his bags and heading for the exit. "Now, let's blow this joint before they change their minds."

As the trio walked out of the store, their arms laden with groceries, Daniel couldn't help but feel a sense of pride. Sure, the world was a messed-up place, but as long as he had his wits and his friends by his side, he knew he could handle whatever it threw at him.

"So," he said, turning to Alice and Kyle with a mischievous grin. "Who's up for a little celebration? I've got a bottle of contraband whiskey burning a hole in my pocket."

Alice and Kyle exchanged a glance, their eyes sparkling with excitement. "Lead the way," Alice said, linking her arm through Daniel's. "After the day we've had, I think we've earned it."

And with that, the three friends set off into the gritty, neon-lit streets of the city, ready to take on whatever challenges lay ahead. Because in a world gone mad, sometimes all you could do was laugh in the face of absurdity and keep on keeping on.

As they made their way down the crowded sidewalk, dodging piles of garbage and suspicious-looking puddles, Daniel couldn't help but chuckle to himself. The absurdity of their situation was almost too much to bear. Here they were, three young rebels, armed with nothing but their wits and a bottle of bootleg booze, ready to take on the world.

Suddenly, Daniel's foot caught on a loose piece of bureaucratic red tape, sending him stumbling forward. His bags went flying, their contents scattering across the filthy pavement. Alice and Kyle, caught off guard, found themselves tangled in the tape, their limbs flailing comically as they tried to free themselves.

"Well, isn't this just perfect," Daniel grumbled, picking himself up and dusting off his jacket. "Even when we win, we lose."

Alice, still struggling to untangle herself, let out a snort of laughter. "That's the way it goes in this world, isn't it? One step forward, two steps back."

Kyle, having finally freed himself, began gathering up their fallen groceries. "At least we've got each other," he said, his voice uncharacteristically sincere. "In a world like this, that counts for something."

Daniel and Alice exchanged a glance, their expressions softening. Kyle was right. They might be just three small cogs in a giant, dysfunctional machine, but together, they were unstoppable.

"Come on," Daniel said, slinging his arm around Kyle's shoulders. "Let's get out of here before the bureaucrats catch wind of our little mishap."

As they walked away, leaving the red tape and scattered groceries behind, Alice couldn't help but smile. "You know," she said, "sometimes I think the only thing keeping me sane in this crazy world is you two."

Daniel grinned, pulling her close. "That's because we're the only ones crazy enough to keep fighting," he said. "And as long as we've got each other, we'll never stop."

And with that, the three friends disappeared into the night, their laughter echoing through the empty streets. The world might be a mess, but as long as they had each other, they knew they could face anything.

Daniel scratched his ass and yawned as he flopped onto the threadbare couch, causing a cloud of Cheeto dust to puff into the air. He grabbed the remote and started flipping through channels, his glazed eyes barely registering the parade of badly-scripted infomercials and lowest-common-denominator reality shows.

Suddenly, the screen flashed to a live news report. A harried-looking anchor babbled excitedly into the camera. "Breaking news! Billionaire Brayden Funkledor has just announced his candidacy for President!"

The screen cut to footage of an enormously fat man waddling up to a podium, his multiple chins wobbling as he waved jovially to the cheering crowd. Daniel sat up straighter, his numb mind struggling to process what he was seeing.

"What the actual fuck?" he muttered. "That tub of lard is running for President? Is this a joke?"

Brayden launched into a bombastic, nonsensical speech, punctuated by wild gesticulations of his pudgy hands. The crowd went wild, chanting his name. Daniel gaped at the TV in slack-jawed disbelief.

"Am I high right now? I must be fucking high," he said, rubbing his eyes. But no, the grotesque spectacle continued to play out in front of him. Brayden prattled on, spouting empty platitudes and blatantly false promises.

Daniel's mind reeled as he tried to make sense of it. How could anyone take this clown seriously as a candidate? Had the country really sunk this low? He shook his head, a grim chuckle escaping his lips.

"We are so fucked," he said to the empty room. "Royally, irredeemably fucked." He reached for another handful of stale Cheetos, shoving them mechanically into his mouth as he continued to watch the surreal scene unfolding on the screen, a growing sense of dread settling in the pit of his stomach.

As the speech continued, Brayden's promises grew more and more outlandish. "We're going to build a wall, folks!" he bellowed, his jowls quivering with enthusiasm. "A big, beautiful wall made of the finest American cheese! It'll keep out the lactose-intolerant immigrants and make our nation grate again!"

Daniel nearly choked on his Cheetos. "A cheese wall? Is this guy for real?" He leaned forward, morbidly fascinated by the sheer absurdity of it all.

Brayden waddled back and forth across the stage, his sweat-stained shirt straining against his massive gut. "And that's not all, my fellow Americans," he continued, his piggy eyes gleaming with excitement. "When I'm President, we'll implement a mandatory 'Dumbocracy'! No more of this elitist intelligence nonsense. In Brayden's America, ignorance will be celebrated! Stupidity will be a virtue!"

The crowd erupted in cheers, waving signs with slogans like "Dumb is the new smart" and "Brayden for Dumbocracy." Daniel felt a wave of nausea wash over him. Was this really the future of his country? A nation ruled by the willfully ignorant, led by a walking, talking caricature of everything wrong with society?

The news anchor appeared on the screen, her perfect teeth gleaming as she gushed over Brayden's speech. "And there you have it, folks! Brayden Funkledor, the candidate who's not afraid to embrace his inner idiot. Let's hear from some of his supporters in the crowd."

The camera cut to a group of people wearing "Brayden for Dumbocracy" t-shirts, their faces contorted in expressions of vacant enthusiasm. "Brayden speaks to me, you know?" one of them said, scratching his head. "He's just like us. He ain't one of them fancy book-learners with their big words and fancy ideas."

Another supporter chimed in, her eyes glazed over with adoration. "Brayden's gonna make America dumb again! We don't need no education, we just need Brayden!"

Daniel felt a hysterical laugh bubbling up in his throat. It was all too much, too absurd to be real. And yet, there it was, playing out right in front of him. A nation on the brink of madness, ready to elect a man who embodied the very worst of humanity.

He reached for the remote, his hand shaking slightly. He needed to turn it off, to escape from this nightmarish reality, if only for a moment.

But even as his finger hovered over the power button, he found himself unable to look away, transfixed by the spectacle of a society teetering on the edge of collapse.

A sharp knock on the door jolted Daniel from his trance. He turned to see Alice and Kyle, their faces mirroring the same bewildered expression he knew was plastered across his own.

"Did you see—" Alice began, but Daniel cut her off with a nod.

"The cheese wall and the Dumbocracy? Yeah, I saw it."

Kyle flopped down on the couch beside Daniel, his eyes still glued to the TV screen. "This can't be real, right? I mean, it's gotta be some kind of sick joke."

Daniel shook his head. "I don't think so, man. Look at those supporters. They're eating this shit up."

The trio fell silent, watching as the news anchor droned on about Brayden's latest poll numbers. It was surreal, like something out of a bad dream or a dystopian novel.

Alice spoke up, her voice tinged with a mix of disbelief and disgust. "You know what this means, right? If Brayden wins, it's game over. We might as well just hand in our brains at the door and join the rest of the idiots."

Daniel snorted. "Bold of you to assume we haven't already reached that point."

Kyle leaned forward, his brow furrowed in thought. "But seriously, think about it. If Brayden becomes President, it's not just gonna be four years of stupidity. It's gonna be a whole new era of ignorance and anti-intellectualism. We're talking about a society where being smart is a crime and being dumb is a badge of honor."

The weight of Kyle's words settled over them like a suffocating blanket. Daniel felt a sense of dread creeping up his spine, a sickening realization that their world was on the brink of something truly terrifying.

Christ, it's like we're living in a bad parody of reality, he thought to himself. *Except the punchline is that we're all screwed.*

He glanced at his friends, seeing the same fear and uncertainty etched across their faces. They were the smart ones, the ones who saw through the bullshit and the lies. But in a world where stupidity reigned supreme, what chance did they really have?

Alice's eyes suddenly lit up with a fierce determination. "Screw this," she said, slamming her hand down on the coffee table. "We can't just sit here and watch this happen. We have to do something."

Daniel raised an eyebrow. "Like what? Run for office ourselves? I don't think 'Vote for the Non-Idiots' is gonna be a winning campaign slogan."

"No, you dumbass," Alice retorted, rolling her eyes. "I mean we need to expose the truth behind Brayden's campaign. Show people just how ridiculous and dangerous he really is."

Kyle leaned back, a skeptical look on his face. "And how exactly do we do that? The guy's a walking meme. People love him because he's a joke."

Alice paced the room, her mind racing with possibilities. "We need to fight fire with fire. Or in this case, fight stupidity with even greater stupidity."

Daniel couldn't help but chuckle. "What, like we start our own campaign? 'Vote for the Slightly Less Dumb Candidate'?"

"No, no, no," Alice said, waving her hand dismissively. "We need to infiltrate Brayden's campaign from the inside. Pose as his biggest supporters and then reveal just how insane his ideas really are."

Kyle snorted. "Right, because that's totally not gonna backfire on us at all."

But Daniel was starting to catch on to Alice's train of thought. "No, wait, I think she might be onto something. We could create our own fake campaign ads, but make them so over-the-top ridiculous that people can't help but see through the bullshit."

Alice grinned, a mischievous glint in her eye. "Exactly. We'll promise things like mandatory nap times for all citizens and a national holiday dedicated to eating pizza in your underwear."

Kyle couldn't help but laugh at the absurdity of it all. "And we'll make Brayden look like a goddamn genius in comparison."

This is insane, Daniel thought to himself. *But then again, so is everything else in this fucked-up world.*

He looked at his friends, a newfound sense of purpose burning in his chest. "Alright, let's do it. Let's take down Brayden Funkledor and his army of idiots, one ridiculous campaign promise at a time."

Daniel pulled out his phone, his fingers flying across the screen as he typed out a message to their group chat.

"Attention all fellow intellectuals (and Kyle)," he wrote, ignoring the middle finger Kyle flashed him from across the room. *"It's time to take a stand against the rising tide of stupidity. Meet at my place tomorrow night, 8 pm sharp. Bring your best ideas and your A-game. And maybe some snacks, because overthrowing a dumbocracy works up an appetite."*

He hit send, feeling a rush of adrenaline coursing through his veins. This was it. They were really doing this.

Alice leaned over his shoulder, reading the message with a smirk. "Nice one. I especially like the part about Kyle."

"Hey!" Kyle protested, but there was no real heat behind it. "I resent that. I'll have you know I'm a goddamn genius when it comes to coming up with stupid ideas."

Daniel snorted. "Well, you'll fit right in with Brayden's supporters then."

He watched as the responses started rolling in, each one more enthusiastic than the last.

"Count me in. It's time to fight dumb with dumber."

"I'll bring the pizza. And the underwear."

"Let's do this. Brayden won't know what hit him."

Daniel felt a surge of pride as he read the messages. These were his people. The ones who refused to accept the status quo, who weren't afraid to stand up and fight for what they believed in, even if it meant making complete fools of themselves in the process.

Because sometimes, he thought, *the only way to beat the system is to play by its own absurd rules.*

He looked up at Alice and Kyle, a grin spreading across his face. "Alright, guys. Let's get to work. We've got a dumbocracy to overthrow."

As they dove into planning mode, tossing around increasingly outlandish ideas, Daniel couldn't shake the feeling that they were in over their heads. Sure, they had passion and determination on their side, but Brayden had an army of morons at his beck and call. They needed someone with experience, someone who knew how to navigate the twisted landscape of their dystopian world.

"We need a mentor," Daniel said, interrupting Kyle's suggestion of a cheese-cannon. "Someone who's been through this before, who can guide us through the shitstorm we're about to unleash."

Alice nodded, her brow furrowed in thought. "But who? It's not like there's a shortage of crazy old coots in this city, but most of them are too busy yelling at pigeons to be of any use."

Just then, Daniel's phone buzzed with an incoming call. He glanced at the screen, his eyes widening in surprise. "Holy shit, it's Professor Zander."

"Professor Zander?" Kyle echoed, his voice tinged with awe. "The mad genius who once hacked into the government's cheese reserves and donated it all to the lactose intolerant? That Professor Zander?"

Daniel nodded, his heart pounding as he answered the call. "Professor Zander, I presume?"

"Daniel, my boy!" The voice on the other end was a mix of eccentric enthusiasm and barely-contained chaos. "I heard you and your friends are planning to take on the dumbocracy. I want in."

Daniel exchanged a look of disbelief with Alice and Kyle. "How did you know about that? We just started sending out messages."

"Let's just say I have my ways," Professor Zander replied cryptically. "Meet me at the abandoned cheese factory on the outskirts of town. Midnight. Come alone, and bring a wheel of Gouda. The stinkier, the better."

With that, the line went dead, leaving Daniel staring at his phone in stunned silence.

"Well, that was unexpected," Alice said, breaking the tension. "But also, kind of perfect? I mean, if anyone knows how to fight absurdity with absurdity, it's Professor Zander."

Kyle nodded, a grin spreading across his face. "Plus, he has access to cheese. Lots and lots of cheese."

Daniel took a deep breath, the weight of their mission settling on his shoulders. "Alright, guys. Let's do this. We've got a professor to meet, a dumbocracy to overthrow, and a wheel of Gouda to procure. What could possibly go wrong?"

Everything, a small voice in the back of his mind whispered. *But that's half the fun, isn't it?*

As the trio prepared to leave for their clandestine meeting with Professor Zander, Daniel couldn't help but feel a mix of excitement and trepidation. *This is it,* he thought. *The moment we stop being passive observers and start being active agents of change.*

Alice rummaged through Daniel's fridge, her face scrunched up in concentration. "Do you have any Gouda in here, or do we need to make a cheese run?"

"I think I have some in the back," Daniel replied, pushing aside a container of leftover pizza. "It might be a little past its prime, but that's probably a good thing, right?"

Kyle sniffed the cheese and recoiled. "Oh, it's definitely stinky. Perfect for our purposes."

They gathered their supplies—the pungent wheel of Gouda, a flashlight, and a map of the city's abandoned industrial district—and headed out into the night. The streets were eerily quiet, save for the occasional blare of a Brayden Funkledor campaign ad from a nearby billboard.

"Do you think Professor Zander really has a plan?" Alice asked as they walked, her voice barely above a whisper.

Daniel shrugged. "I don't know, but at this point, I'm willing to try anything. Even if it means meeting a crazy professor in an abandoned cheese factory at midnight."

Kyle clapped him on the shoulder. "That's the spirit! Embrace the madness, my friend. It's the only way to survive in this world."

As they approached the factory, a figure emerged from the shadows, a wild glint in his eye. "Welcome, my young revolutionaries," Professor Zander said, his voice echoing in the empty space. "I see you brought the Gouda. Excellent."

Daniel handed over the cheese, feeling a sense of anticipation building in his chest. "So, what's the plan, Professor?"

Zander's grin was a slash of white in the darkness. "The plan, my dear boy, is to fight fire with fire. Or, in this case, to fight absurdity with absurdity. Brayden Funkledor wants a wall made of cheese? We'll give him a moat made of fondue. He wants a dumbocracy? We'll create a smartocracy, where intelligence and critical thinking reign supreme."

Alice's eyes widened. "But how do we do that?"

"By using their own tactics against them," Zander replied. "We'll launch a counter-campaign, one that's even more ridiculous than Brayden's. We'll rally the masses with our wit, our charm, and our unrelenting commitment to reason."

Kyle raised his hand. "Question: will there be more cheese involved?"

Zander's laughter was a burst of manic energy. "Oh, my boy, there will be cheese. So much cheese. But first, we need to gather our allies and create a plan of attack. Are you with me?"

Daniel looked at Alice and Kyle, saw the determination in their eyes, and felt a swell of pride. *This is our chance,* he thought. *Our chance to make a difference, to change the world.*

He turned to Professor Zander, a fierce grin on his face. "We're with you, Professor. Let's do this."

And with that, the unlikely team of rebels set to work, their minds buzzing with ideas and their hearts full of hope. The dumbocracy wouldn't know what hit it.

Daniel shouldered his way through the throng of Brayden supporters, their mindless chants grating on his last nerve. "Brayden knows best! Put your faith to the test!" they droned, waving signs with slogans like "Ignorance is Strength" and "Freedom is Slavery."

Alice grabbed Daniel's arm. "This is insane. They're like brainwashed zombies."

"Zombies with a serious hard-on for conformity," Kyle quipped, dodging a stray elbow.

Daniel's jaw clenched as he took in the sea of glazed eyes and vacant smiles. These people were so far gone, they'd probably vote for a goddamn turnip if Brayden told them to. But he'd be damned if he let that smug prick lead the country further down the crapper without a fight.

Spotting a rickety stage at the far end of the park, Daniel surged forward with renewed determination. "Come on," he called over his shoulder. "Time to give these sheep a wake-up call."

Alice and Kyle exchanged a look before falling into step beside him, their friends close behind. They reached the stage and Daniel bounded up the steps two at a time. He snatched the microphone from its stand, flicking it on with a screech of feedback that made the nearest Brayden-bots wince.

"Hey! Listen up, you brainwashed bastards!" Daniel's voice boomed across the park. Heads swiveled in his direction and the chanting petered out. He had their attention, for now. Time to make it count.

Daniel cleared his throat, a wry grin spreading across his face as he surveyed the confused faces staring back at him. "I know you're all here because you think Brayden's got the answers, but let me tell you, his campaign promises are about as solid as a wet fart in a hurricane."

A few snickers rippled through the crowd, and Daniel's grin widened. He was getting through to them. "I mean, come on, folks. 'A chicken in every pot and a robot in every garage'? Who comes up with this shit? I'll tell you who: a man who's never had to worry about putting food on the table or keeping a roof over his head."

He paused, letting his words sink in. "Brayden talks a big game about making our lives better, but all he's really doing is blowing smoke up our asses. He's promising the moon and stars, but he's got no plan to deliver. It's all just a bunch of empty slogans and flashy propaganda."

Daniel began to pace the stage, his voice rising with each step. "Take his 'Jobs for All' initiative. Sounds great, right? But what he's not telling you is that those jobs are in his own factories, working for peanuts while he lines his pockets with the profits. And his 'Green New Deal'? More like a 'Green New Steal,' funneling taxpayer money into his cronies' pet projects while the rest of us choke on smog."

He stopped center stage, locking eyes with the crowd. "But the real kicker? His 'Unity Through Diversity' platform. It's a load of crap, and you all know it. Brayden doesn't give a rat's ass about diversity. He just wants to divide us up into neat little boxes so he can pit us against each other and keep us distracted while he consolidates his power."

Daniel's chest heaved as he caught his breath, the crowd murmuring and shifting restlessly. He could see the doubt creeping into their eyes, the first cracks in Brayden's carefully crafted facade.

"Listen, I know you're all looking for someone to believe in, someone who can make sense of this fucked-up world we're living in. But Brayden ain't it. He's just another snake oil salesman, peddling false hope and empty promises. It's time we woke up and started thinking for ourselves, before it's too late."

He let the mic drop to his side, his piece said. The crowd was silent for a long moment, the weight of his words hanging in the air. Then, slowly at first but with gathering momentum, a ripple of applause began to build. It started with a few hesitant claps, then grew into a roar of approval as more and more people joined in.

Daniel glanced back at Alice and Kyle, who were grinning from ear to ear. They'd done it. They'd planted the seeds of doubt, and now it was up to the people to nurture them into a full-blown rebellion. The fight was far from over, but for the first time in a long time, Daniel felt a flicker of hope. Maybe, just maybe, they could take their country back from the likes of Brayden and his ilk. One speech at a time.

As the applause began to die down, Alice, Kyle, and the others sprang into action. They wove through the crowd, pressing flyers and pamphlets into the hands of anyone who would take them. The brightly colored pages were emblazoned with slogans like "Brayden's Lies: Now in Fun-Size!" and "The Truth About Brayden: It's Not Pretty, But It's Pretty Funny!"

Alice handed a flyer to a middle-aged woman wearing a "Brayden's Babes" t-shirt. The woman glanced at the page, her eyes widening as she read the bullet points exposing Brayden's broken promises and half-truths. "Is this for real?" she asked, her voice wavering with uncertainty.

"As real as Brayden's spray tan," Alice quipped, flashing a grin. "But don't take my word for it. Do your own research, and you'll see the truth for yourself."

The woman nodded slowly, folding the flyer and tucking it into her pocket. Alice moved on, her smile growing wider with each person she reached.

Meanwhile, Kyle had struck up a conversation with a group of college-aged guys who had been chanting one of Brayden's slogans moments earlier. "So, let me get this straight," he said, his tone dripping with sarcasm. "You guys actually believe that Brayden's going to 'Make America Grate Again' by banning all foreign cheeses?"

The guys exchanged uncertain glances, their brows furrowed in confusion. "Well, when you put it that way..." one of them mumbled, scratching his head.

"Exactly," Kyle said, pressing a pamphlet into the guy's hand. "Brayden's full of shit, and it's time we all woke up and smelled the limburger."

As Alice, Kyle, and the others continued to work the crowd, Daniel watched with a growing sense of pride. He could see the wheels turning in people's minds, the doubt and skepticism taking root. It was a small victory, but it was a start.

And then, just as the energy seemed to be shifting in their favor, a voice rang out from the back of the crowd. "Don't listen to these losers!" it shouted, cutting through the din. "Brayden's the only one who can save us from the chaos!"

Daniel's heart sank as he recognized the voice. It was one of Brayden's most ardent supporters, a man known for his blind loyalty and his penchant for stirring up trouble. The man pushed his way to the front of the crowd, his face twisted in a sneer.

"You think you're so clever, don't you?" he spat, jabbing a finger at Daniel. "With your fancy words and your so-called 'truth.' Well, I've got news for you, pal. The only truth that matters is the one that Brayden tells us. And if you can't see that, then you're just another part of the problem."

The crowd began to murmur and shift, the earlier sense of unity fracturing under the weight of the man's words. Daniel glanced at Alice and Kyle, who looked back at him with grim determination. They knew the battle was just beginning, and they were ready to fight tooth and nail for what they believed in.

But as the man continued to rant and rave, his words growing more nonsensical by the second, Daniel felt a flicker of hope. Because even as the crowd began to splinter and divide, he could see the truth shining through in the eyes of those who had been swayed by his message. And he knew that no matter how long it took, no matter how hard they had to fight, the truth would always win out in the end.

Daniel gripped the microphone tighter, his knuckles turning white as he stared down the heckler. The man's face was red with anger, his eyes bulging as he shouted, "Brayden is the only one who can save us from this hellhole! You're just a bunch of traitors trying to undermine him!"

A few scattered cheers rose from the crowd, but they were quickly drowned out by a chorus of boos and hisses. Daniel's supporters rallied around him, their voices rising in a defiant chant: "Lies, lies, Brayden lies! Open up your damn eyes!"

The heckler's face twisted into an ugly sneer. "You think you're funny? You think this is some kind of joke? Well, let me tell you something - Brayden's the only one who can keep us safe from the mutant squirrels and the radioactive zombies. Without him, we're all screwed!"

Daniel couldn't help but laugh. "Mutant squirrels? Radioactive zombies? Are you serious right now? Brayden's been feeding you a load of bullshit, and you're just lapping it up like a thirsty dog."

The crowd erupted into laughter and applause, and Daniel felt a surge of confidence. He turned to face the rest of the audience, his voice ringing out clear and strong. "Listen up, everyone. Brayden's been lying to you. He's not some kind of savior or hero. He's just a power-hungry jackass who'll say anything to get what he wants."

As Daniel spoke, more and more people began to nod their heads in agreement. A few even stepped forward to join him on the stage, their own stories of disillusionment and frustration pouring out in a torrent of anger and betrayal.

But the hecklers weren't about to give up so easily. They surged forward, their faces contorted with rage as they screamed and shouted over Daniel's words. "Traitors! Liars! You'll pay for this!"

Daniel steeled himself for the fight ahead, knowing that it wouldn't be easy to break through the wall of ignorance and blind loyalty that Brayden had built up over the years. But he also knew that he had truth on his side - and that was a weapon more powerful than any mutant squirrel or radioactive zombie could ever hope to be.

As the chaos intensified, Daniel's friends rallied around him, forming a protective circle on the stage. Alice stepped forward, her voice cutting through the din like a knife. "You want to talk about lies? How about the lie that Brayden actually cares about any of you? He's just using you for his own gain!"

Kyle chimed in, his tone dripping with sarcasm. "Yeah, and what about that promise to give everyone a free lifetime supply of neon green sludge? I'm sure that'll solve all our problems!"

The hecklers faltered, their chants growing less confident as they looked to each other in confusion. Daniel seized the moment, his voice booming out over the crowd. "Wake up, people! Brayden's not the answer. He's just another part of the problem. But together, we can find a better way. A way that doesn't involve blindly following some egomaniac with a bad haircut and a worse attitude."

The crowd began to murmur, the tide slowly turning in Daniel's favor. Some of the hecklers even began to look ashamed, their signs and banners drooping as they realized the truth behind his words.

But there were still those who clung stubbornly to their beliefs, their faces twisted with anger and denial. They surged forward, determined to bring Daniel down by any means necessary.

Daniel braced himself, knowing that the battle was far from over. But as he looked out over the sea of faces, he saw something that gave him hope. A glimmer of understanding, a spark of rebellion. And he knew that no matter what happened next, he had started something that could not be stopped.

Daniel grinned, sensing the momentum shifting in his favor. He turned to the crowd, his eyes sparkling with mischief. "Hey, everyone! Let's give Brayden a chant he'll never forget!"

He began to clap his hands in a catchy rhythm, his voice ringing out over the park. "Brayden's promises, they're all lies! Watch out, folks, he's in disguise!"

Alice, Kyle, and the others quickly joined in, their voices blending together in a humorous harmony. The crowd hesitated for a moment, then slowly began to clap along, their faces breaking into smiles as they caught on to the satirical chant.

"He'll promise you the moon and stars, but all you'll get are broken cars!" Daniel continued, his voice growing louder with each line. "Brayden's campaign, it's just a scam, don't be fooled by his Instagram!"

The chant spread like wildfire, the disillusioned masses joining in with gusto. Even some of the die-hard Brayden supporters found themselves tapping their feet and nodding along, unable to resist the catchy tune and biting lyrics.

As the chant reached a crescendo, Daniel leaped off the stage, high-fiving his friends with a triumphant grin. They laughed and joked as they made their way through the crowd, basking in the newfound energy and support.

"Did you see their faces?" Alice chuckled, her eyes bright with excitement. "I thought that one guy's head was going to explode when you started the chant!"

"Yeah, well, someone had to knock some sense into them," Daniel smirked, his heart racing with adrenaline. "And let's be real, my rhymes are pretty damn irresistible."

Kyle rolled his eyes, but couldn't hide his grin. "Alright, Mr. Irresistible, let's not get ahead of ourselves. We've still got a long way to go if we want to take down Brayden."

Daniel nodded, his expression growing serious for a moment. "You're right. But today, we showed them that we're not going down without a fight. And with this kind of support, I know we can win."

As they left the park, Daniel couldn't help but feel a surge of hope and determination. They had started something big, something that could change the course of their dystopian world. And he knew that no matter what challenges lay ahead, he and his friends would face them head-on, armed with their wit, their courage, and their unbreakable bond.

Daniel and his friends pushed open the door to the Quantum Leap Café, a cacophony of clashing colors and quirky decor assaulting their senses. Mismatched furniture in eye-searing hues filled the space, while abstract paintings hung crookedly on the walls. A customer lounged on a plush armchair, wearing a tinfoil hat and mumbling conspiracy theories into his coffee mug.

"Are we in the right place?" Lila whispered, eyeing a taxidermied squirrel wearing a top hat and monocle.

Daniel smirked. "Definitely seems like Zander's scene."

They wove through the eclectic seating area, dodging a waiter on a pogo stick balancing a tray of rainbow-colored scones. Daniel wondered what kind of mind-altering substances were baked into the iridescent pastries. Probably best not to ask.

Suddenly, the café doors burst open with a dramatic flourish. Professor Zander strode in, a whirlwind of clashing patterns and vibrant colors. They wore a neon green tailcoat, paired with orange polka-dot pants and a purple top hat adorned with a stuffed parrot.

A stack of teetering books was tucked under one arm, titles like "The Art of Subversive Snark" and "Overthrowing Oppressors with Witty One-Liners" visible on the spines.

"Darlings!" Zander exclaimed, their voice booming through the café. "So delighted you could join me in this haven of absurdity!"

All eyes turned to the eccentric figure, some patrons gawking openly while others simply shrugged, unfazed by the spectacle. Daniel grinned, feeling a surge of excitement. If anyone could help them navigate this dystopian shitshow, it was Zander.

Zander sashayed towards their table, the parrot bobbing precariously on their hat. They plopped the stack of books down with a resounding thud and spread their arms wide in a theatrical gesture.

"Welcome, my unconventional protégés, to the beginning of your subversive education! Prepare to have your minds blown and your wit sharpened to a razor's edge."

Daniel leaned forward eagerly, ready to absorb whatever unorthodox wisdom Zander had to impart. In a world gone mad, embracing the absurd seemed like the only sane choice. And with Zander as their guide, they might just stand a chance of out-weirding the powers that be.

Daniel approached Professor Zander, determination etched on his face. "Professor, we're here because we want to challenge this ridiculous status quo. We need your guidance to navigate this clusterfuck of a society."

Zander's eyes twinkled with mischief. "Ah, young Daniel, seeking to unravel the mysteries of our absurd existence? Well, buckle up, buttercup, because you're in for a wild ride!"

The professor's cryptic remark only fueled Daniel's curiosity. What kind of wild ride were they in for? He exchanged glances with his friends, their expressions a mix of excitement and trepidation.

As the group gathered around the table, Zander leaned back in their chair, propping their feet up on a pile of books. "Now, let me regale you with tales of our dystopian wonderland, where common sense is as rare as a unicorn in a business suit."

Zander launched into a series of humorous anecdotes, each one more outrageous than the last. "Take the Department of Redundancy Department, for example. They've decreed that every citizen must fill out a form to request a form to fill out. It's a never-ending cycle of bureaucratic bullshit!"

The group couldn't help but chuckle at the absurdity of it all. Daniel found himself nodding along, recognizing the frustrating hoops they had to jump through daily.

"And don't even get me started on the fashion police," Zander continued, gesturing to their own eclectic outfit. "They once tried to arrest me for 'crimes against color coordination.' Can you believe it? In a world where conformity is king, a little sartorial rebellion goes a long way!"

Zander's words struck a chord with Daniel. In a society that demanded uniformity, embracing one's individuality was an act of defiance. He glanced at his friends, their own unique styles standing out like beacons of hope in a sea of monotony.

As Zander regaled them with more tales of bureaucratic absurdity and societal shenanigans, Daniel felt a growing sense of camaraderie. They weren't alone in their desire to challenge the status quo. With Zander's guidance and their own determination, they might just stand a chance of bringing some sanity to this mad, mad world.

Professor Zander leaned forward, a mischievous glint in their eye. "Now, my dear rebels, let me share with you some unconventional strategies for dealing with Brayden's supporters."

The group huddled closer, eager to hear the professor's wisdom. Daniel couldn't help but feel a surge of excitement, knowing that Zander's methods were bound to be as unorthodox as they were effective.

"First and foremost," Zander began, "never underestimate the power of humor and satire. When faced with the absurdity of their arguments, respond with wit and clever retorts. It throws them off balance and exposes the ridiculousness of their beliefs."

Daniel nodded, recalling a recent encounter with a particularly fervent Brayden supporter. "I once had someone tell me that Brayden's plan to replace all books with picture books was a stroke of genius," he shared, rolling his eyes. "I couldn't help but ask if they were planning on coloring outside the lines as an act of rebellion."

The group erupted in laughter, and Zander clapped their hands in approval. "Exactly! That's the spirit. Subversion through humor is a powerful tool. It's like using a whoopee cushion to deflate their inflated egos."

As the laughter subsided, Zander's expression turned more serious. "But remember, it's not just about cracking jokes. It's about challenging the status quo, thinking outside the box, and finding creative ways to resist."

They reached into their pocket and pulled out a handful of small, colorful buttons. "Take these, for example," Zander said, distributing them among the group. "Each button contains a scandalous message hidden beneath a layer of scratch-off paint. Wear them proudly, and when someone questions you, invite them to scratch off the surface and reveal the truth beneath."

Daniel examined his button, a smile tugging at his lips. The idea of hiding subversive messages in plain sight was both thrilling and ingenious. He couldn't wait to see the reactions of Brayden's supporters when they uncovered the truth.

As the meeting continued, the group shared their own experiences and frustrations with Brayden's followers. They exchanged stories of ridiculous encounters, each one more absurd than the last.

"I once had a guy tell me that Brayden's plan to replace all food with nutrient-fortified sludge was a brilliant solution to world hunger,"

Daniel's friend, Sarah, shared. "I asked him if he'd be willing to be the first to take a sip from the sludge fountain. Suddenly, he wasn't so enthusiastic anymore."

Professor Zander chuckled, shaking their head. "Ah, the hypocrisy of it all. They're quick to advocate for nonsensical policies, but heaven forbid they have to live with the consequences themselves."

The conversation flowed freely, punctuated by laughter and moments of shared understanding. In the midst of the absurdity, Daniel found solace in the knowledge that he wasn't alone in his fight against the dystopian madness.

As the meeting drew to a close, Professor Zander stood up, a twinkle in their eye. "Remember, my dear rebels, laughter is the best medicine. Well, that and a healthy dose of civil disobedience. So go forth, armed with your wit and your conviction, and show those Brayden supporters that we won't go down without a chuckle!"

With renewed determination and a sense of camaraderie, Daniel and his friends bid farewell to Professor Zander, ready to face the absurdities of their world head-on. They knew that the road ahead would be filled with challenges, but they also knew that they had the power of humor and subversion on their side. And in a world gone mad, that was the most potent weapon of all.

Professor Zander leaned forward, a mischievous glint in their eyes. "Now, my dear troublemakers, it's time to embrace your inner quirks and use them as weapons against the absurdity of this dystopian hellscape."

Daniel raised an eyebrow. "Our quirks? You mean like my uncanny ability to make puns at the most inappropriate times?"

"Precisely!" Professor Zander exclaimed. "Your unique strengths, no matter how unconventional, can be used to dismantle the nonsensical arguments of Brayden's supporters. Fight absurdity with absurdity, I always say."

Laughter erupted from the group, and Daniel felt a surge of excitement. The idea of wielding his quirks as a weapon was both thrilling and ridiculous.

Professor Zander stood up abruptly, a wicked grin on their face. "Allow me to demonstrate." They cleared their throat and assumed an exaggerated posture. "As a proud supporter of Brayden, I believe that we should mandate the consumption of green Jell-O at every meal. It's the key to a healthy and obedient population!"

The group stared at Professor Zander, dumbfounded by the absurd claim. Daniel's mind raced, searching for a witty comeback. "Well, I propose we counter that by requiring everyone to wear mismatched socks. It'll promote individuality and chaos, the perfect antidote to your Jell-O dystopia!"

Professor Zander clapped their hands, beaming with pride. "Brilliant! You're getting the hang of it. Now, let's see what the rest of you can come up with."

The café burst into a frenzy of laughter and absurd counterclaims. Each member of the group took turns playing the role of a Brayden supporter, spouting increasingly ridiculous arguments, while the others fired back with their own brand of satirical wit.

As the exercise continued, Daniel felt a sense of liberation wash over him. For the first time in a long while, he felt like he had the power to fight back against the madness that had consumed their world.

Professor Zander watched the group with a satisfied smirk, their eyes twinkling with mischief. "You see? When you embrace your quirks and use them to expose the absurdity of their arguments, you take away their power. Laughter is the ultimate rebellion in a world that has lost its sense of humor."

Daniel nodded, a newfound determination coursing through his veins. He glanced around at his friends, seeing the same fire in their eyes. They were ready to take on the dystopian landscape, armed with their unique strengths and a healthy dose of irreverence.

Professor Zander leaned back in their chair, a satisfied grin on their face. "Now, let's talk strategy. I have a few ideas on how we can really shake things up and make those Brayden supporters question their own sanity."

The group huddled closer, eager to hear more of Professor Zander's unconventional wisdom. In that moment, Daniel knew that they had found more than just an eccentric mentor - they had found a kindred spirit in the fight against the absurdities of their world.

Daniel and his friends huddled around a cluttered table, their eyes glued to the screens of their devices as Professor Zander paced behind them, a manic grin on their face. "Alright, my little rebels, it's time to dive into the cesspool of social media echo chambers and learn how to navigate the nonsensical political jargon that plagues our dystopian society!"

The professor leaned over Daniel's shoulder, pointing at a particularly convoluted post. "You see this? It's a prime example of the verbal diarrhea that Brayden's supporters spew on a daily basis. Let's break it down, shall we?"

As Professor Zander dissected the post, highlighting the absurdity of the claims and the circular logic employed, the group couldn't help but burst into laughter. Daniel's friend, Sarah, snorted, "It's like they're playing a game of 'who can make the least sense' and winning every time!"

The training session continued, with Professor Zander guiding them through the labyrinth of political doublespeak and propaganda. They taught the group how to identify logical fallacies, spot manipulation techniques, and craft witty retorts that exposed the ridiculousness of the arguments.

Daniel found himself energized by the process, his mind buzzing with newfound strategies and comebacks. He couldn't wait to put them into practice and watch the confusion and frustration on the faces of Brayden's supporters.

As the session wound down, Professor Zander shared a few humorous anecdotes from their own experiences challenging the dystopian society. "I once infiltrated a Brayden rally dressed as a giant banana," they recounted, eyes twinkling with mischief. "I stood there, holding a sign that read 'Peel back the lies,' and watched as they tried to make sense of it. The looks on their faces were priceless!"

The group howled with laughter, imagining the absurdity of the scene. Daniel couldn't help but admire Professor Zander's audacity and commitment to the cause.

"Remember, my dear rebels," Professor Zander said, their tone turning serious for a moment, "persistence and resilience are key. They will try to wear you down, to make you question your own sanity. But you must stay strong, stay focused, and never lose your sense of humor. It's the most powerful weapon we have against the absurdity of this world."

Daniel nodded, feeling a renewed sense of purpose. He glanced around at his friends, seeing the determination etched on their faces. They were ready to take on the challenges ahead, armed with their wits, their humor, and the knowledge that they were not alone in this fight.

As the group packed up their belongings and prepared to leave the café, Daniel couldn't help but feel a sense of excitement for what lay ahead. With Professor Zander's guidance and the support of his friends, he knew that they could make a difference, one absurd encounter at a time.

Professor Zander leaned back in their chair, a mischievous glint in their eye. "And one last thing, my young padawans of satire," they said, their voice dropping to a conspiratorial whisper. "Never underestimate the power of laughter. It's the kryptonite to their nonsense, the light saber to their dark side. Wield it with precision, and watch as the absurdity crumbles around them."

Daniel exchanged a grin with his friends, feeling the weight of Professor Zander's words. He knew that the road ahead would be filled with challenges, with moments of frustration and doubt. But he also knew that they had the tools to face it head-on, to expose the flaws and contradictions of Brayden's supporters with a well-timed joke or a clever meme.

As they stood up to leave, Professor Zander engulfed each of them in a warm hug, their mismatched outfit rustling with each embrace. "Remember, my dear rebels," they said, their voice filled with pride, "you are the future. You are the ones who will shape this world, one laugh at a time. Now go forth and spread the gospel of satire!"

With a final salute and a flourish, Professor Zander spun on their heel and sauntered out of the café, leaving a trail of amused and bewildered looks in their wake.

Daniel and his friends lingered for a moment, savoring the energy and inspiration that Professor Zander had imparted. They knew that the journey ahead would be filled with twists and turns, with moments of triumph and setbacks. But they also knew that they had each other, a band of misfits united by their love of laughter and their determination to make a difference.

As they stepped out into the streets, the absurdity of the world seemed to shimmer around them, ripe with possibilities for satire and subversion. Daniel felt a grin spreading across his face, his mind already buzzing with ideas for their next move.

This is going to be one hell of a ride, he thought to himself, exchanging a knowing look with his friends. *And I wouldn't have it any other way.*

Daniel stepped into the dilapidated warehouse, his eyes adjusting to the dim light that filtered through the grimy windows. Around him, bizarre contraptions and props littered the space - a giant hamster wheel, a stack of mismatched traffic cones, and what appeared to be a deconstructed clown car.

Alice and Kyle trailed behind him, their footsteps echoing off the concrete floor. Their other friends had already gathered in the makeshift training area, perched on wobbly folding chairs and leaning against rusted metal beams.

"What kind of crackpot operation are they running here?" Alice muttered, kicking aside a deflated rubber chicken.

Daniel snorted. Between the nutjob political propaganda and now this freak show setup, he was starting to wonder if they'd stepped into some kind of surrealist nightmare. Then again, with Brayden Funkledor running things these days, surreal was the new normal.

The screech of hinges made them spin around. A side door burst open and in swept a tall figure draped in clashing neon patterns. A hat topped with feathers bobbed precariously on his head as he sashayed towards them.

"Welcome, welcome!" the man trilled, arms spread wide. With a flourish of his wrist, he whipped off the hat and bowed deeply. "I am the incomparable, the enigmatic, the utterly astonishing... Professor Zander!"

He popped up and plopped the hat back on his head, beaming at them expectantly. Daniel exchanged a sideways glance with Kyle, who looked like he was trying very hard not to bust out laughing.

"Uh, hey there, Prof," Daniel said, fighting to keep a straight face. "Nice getup. Raided a clown's closet on the way here?"

"Pish posh! I'll have you know this ensemble was hand-selected to stimulate your brains and ignite your creativity!" Zander wagged a finger at them. "Now, gather round, my pupils. Your eccentric yet devastatingly brilliant mentor has much to impart..."

As the motley group circled around the professor, Daniel couldn't help but grin. This ought to be good. If Zander's fashion sense was any indicator, they were in for one wild ride. He leaned in, ready to see what kind of craziness their new teacher had in store.

Professor Zander whipped out a stack of papers from his gaudy jacket and fanned them out like a magician revealing a card trick. "Behold! Your first challenge awaits!"

He handed each of them a sheaf of pages covered in dense, convoluted text. Daniel squinted at the jumble of words, his brow furrowing. It looked like someone had tossed a dictionary into a blender and hit puree.

"What the hell is this?" Kyle muttered, flipping through his pages. "It's like a mad lib on steroids."

"Ah, but that's the beauty of it!" Zander exclaimed, his eyes twinkling with mischief. "Your task, my dear students, is to decipher the hidden meaning lurking within this nonsensical political jargon. Dig deep, read between the lines, and uncover the truth that lies beneath!"

Alice snorted, holding up a page. "I'm pretty sure this is just a bunch of buzzwords strung together. 'Synergistic paradigm shift'? 'Holistic strategic alignment'? It's like corporate bingo in here."

"Exactly!" Zander clapped his hands, looking positively delighted. "The art of political doublespeak is a wily beast, but I have faith that you'll tame it in no time. Now, dive in and let the absurdity wash over you!"

Daniel shook his head, a grin tugging at his lips. He had to hand it to the prof - this was definitely a unique approach to training. He glanced around at his friends, who were already huddling together and poring over the pages with a mix of confusion and amusement.

"Okay, I think I got something," Kyle announced, jabbing a finger at his paper. "'Leveraging cross-functional synergies for optimal outcomes' - that's gotta mean 'teamwork,' right?"

"Nah, man," Daniel countered, squinting at his own page. "I'm pretty sure it's more like 'making shit up as you go and hoping it works out.'"

Alice let out a bark of laughter. "I vote for Daniel's interpretation. It's way more accurate."

As they traded theories and interpretations, the warehouse filled with the sounds of laughter and good-natured ribbing. Daniel leaned back, soaking in the camaraderie. Sure, the world outside might be a dystopian hellscape, but in moments like these, he felt like they could take on anything.

Professor Zander watched them with a proud smile, his mismatched outfit seeming more endearing than ridiculous now. "Excellent work, my young padawans! You're well on your way to mastering the art of deciphering political bullshit. Keep at it, and soon you'll be able to see through even the thickest smokescreen of bureaucratic babble!"

Daniel grinned, feeling a surge of determination. Bring it on, he thought. With his friends by his side and a crazy mentor like Zander, he was ready to take on whatever this twisted world threw at them. One nonsensical phrase at a time.

Daniel frowned at the next paragraph, the words blurring together into an incomprehensible mess. "I swear, this one's just a random word generator threw up on the page."

Professor Zander peered over his shoulder, nodding sagely. "Ah, yes. The classic 'throw everything at the wall and see what sticks' approach. A favorite among politicians who have no idea what they're talking about."

"Which is pretty much all of them," Alice quipped, eliciting a round of snickers from the group.

As they continued to wade through the quagmire of political jargon, Professor Zander circulated among them, offering his unique brand of guidance.

"Remember, my dear students," he said, his voice taking on a theatrical quality, "the key to understanding this nonsense is to embrace the absurdity. Don't try to make sense of it; instead, look for the hidden agendas, the smoke and mirrors, the sheer audacity of their bullshittery!"

Daniel nodded, a smirk tugging at his lips. He had to hand it to the old man; he had a way of making even the most tedious tasks feel like a subversive act of rebellion.

Hours passed, and the group's initial enthusiasm began to wane. Kyle had resorted to folding his papers into elaborate origami shapes, while Alice doodled unflattering caricatures of politicians in the margins of her notes.

Just as Daniel was about to suggest a break, a particular phrase caught his eye. He read it once, then twice, his brow furrowing in concentration.

"Guys," he said slowly, "I think I found something."

The others looked up, curiosity piqued.

"Listen to this: 'The fluorescent green initiative will revolutionize the industry by harnessing the power of invisible pink unicorns.' It's not just nonsense; it's a code!"

Professor Zander clapped his hands, his eyes sparkling with mischief. "Bravo, Daniel! You've cracked the first layer of their deception. Now, dig deeper! What do you think they're really trying to say?"

Daniel studied the page, his mind racing. "The 'fluorescent green initiative' could be a cover for some kind of shady deal, and the 'invisible pink unicorns' might represent the illicit funds or resources they're using to make it happen."

The group erupted in a chorus of "ooh"s and "ahh"s, their enthusiasm reignited.

"Daniel, you're a genius!" Alice exclaimed, punching him playfully on the arm.

Professor Zander beamed, his pride evident. "Well done, my boy. You've taken your first step towards becoming a true master of decoding political bullshit. Keep this up, and you'll be running circles around those bureaucratic bastards in no time!"

As the group celebrated Daniel's breakthrough, he couldn't help but feel a sense of pride. Sure, the world was still a mess, and they had a long way to go, but moments like these made him believe that they could actually make a difference.

With renewed energy, they dove back into the task at hand, ready to unravel the next layer of political absurdity. Daniel grinned, feeling more alive than he had in years. This, he thought, is what rebellion feels like.

Professor Zander clapped his hands, drawing the group's attention. "Alright, my intrepid truth-seekers, it's time to take this party to the next level. Welcome to the wild world of social media echo chambers!"

He whipped out a set of sleek, black headsets from a battered cardboard box. "These bad boys will transport you to a virtual hellscape filled with enough conspiracy theories and misinformation to make your heads spin. Your mission, should you choose to accept it, is to navigate through the chaos and come out the other side with your sanity intact."

Kyle raised an eyebrow. "You want us to willingly subject ourselves to that madness?"

"Think of it as an immunization against the bullshit," Professor Zander replied with a wink. "Besides, where's the fun in playing it safe?"

The group exchanged apprehensive glances, but their curiosity won out. They each grabbed a headset and slipped them on, bracing themselves for the unknown.

As the virtual world materialized around them, Daniel found himself standing in a neon-lit alleyway, surrounded by towering skyscrapers plastered with flickering screens. The air buzzed with a cacophony of voices, each one shouting louder than the last.

"Holy shit, it's like Times Square on acid," Alice muttered, her eyes wide behind the headset.

They cautiously made their way down the alley, dodging virtual pedestrians who seemed more interested in their glowing devices than their surroundings. Suddenly, a holographic figure materialized in front of them, a wild-eyed man with a tinfoil hat.

"The lizard people are controlling the weather!" he screeched, thrusting a virtual pamphlet into their faces. "Wake up, sheeple!"

Daniel couldn't help but laugh at the absurdity of it all. "Thanks, but I think I'll pass on the lizard people today."

As they pressed on, the theories grew more outlandSorry, I got cut off there. Here's the continuation:

As they pressed on, the theories grew more outlandish by the minute. Flat earth, faked moon landings, and government-controlled pigeons - it was a veritable buffet of absurdity.

"I feel like I'm losing brain cells by the second," Kyle groaned, swatting away a holographic chemtrail.

Alice, however, seemed to be in her element. She engaged the virtual conspiracy theorists in lively debates, poking holes in their logic with surgical precision.

"If the earth is flat, how come we have time zones, huh? Riddle me that!" she challenged a particularly passionate flat-earther.

The virtual avatar sputtered, his argument crumbling under the weight of Alice's relentless questioning.

Daniel watched in awe as Alice tore through the echo chambers like a hot knife through butter. He couldn't help but admire her quick wit and unwavering determination.

"Damn, Alice," he chuckled, "you're like the Terminator of bullshit."

She flashed him a grin. "I've had plenty of practice dealing with my crazy uncle's Facebook posts."

As they delved deeper into the virtual landscape, the absurdity reached fever pitch. Holograms spouting increasingly bizarre theories swarmed around them, their voices blending into a discordant symphony of nonsense.

Daniel felt his head spinning, the lines between reality and fiction blurring with each passing moment. But amidst the chaos, he found solace in the camaraderie of his friends. Together, they laughed in the face of the madness, their bond growing stronger with every ridiculous encounter.

And as they finally emerged from the virtual echo chambers, dizzy but triumphant, Daniel realized that perhaps the key to surviving in this dystopian world wasn't just about debunking the lies - it was about finding the people who would stand by your side and face the absurdity head-on.

Kyle's fingers danced across the virtual keyboard, his eyes darting between lines of code as he navigated through the digital labyrinth. The echo chambers morphed and shifted around him, adapting to his every move.

"It's like playing the world's most twisted game of Pac-Man," he muttered, his brow furrowed in concentration.

Daniel watched as Kyle manipulated the virtual environment, redirecting conspiracy theories and diverting the flow of misinformation. It was like watching a master conductor orchestrating a symphony of chaos.

"How the hell do you do that?" Daniel asked, his voice tinged with equal parts admiration and bewilderment.

Kyle flashed him a mischievous grin. "Years of practice hacking into my school's computer system to change my grades."

Daniel shook his head, a smile tugging at the corners of his mouth. "Remind me never to piss you off."

As they pressed on, the virtual world grew increasingly surreal. Memes came to life, viral videos played on endless loops, and the very fabric of reality seemed to warp and bend to the whims of the algorithm.

But with each challenge, the group's skills sharpened. They learned to question everything, to dig deeper beneath the surface of the absurdity. They became digital detectives, unraveling the threads of misinformation and exposing the truth hidden beneath.

And as the final conspiracy theory crumbled under the weight of their scrutiny, Daniel felt a sense of pride swell within him. They had done more than just survive the echo chambers - they had conquered them.

He glanced around at his friends, their faces etched with a mix of exhaustion and exhilaration. In that moment, he knew that together, they could face anything this dystopian world could throw at them.

As they removed their virtual reality headsets, blinking as their eyes adjusted to the dim light of the warehouse, Professor Zander greeted them with a slow clap.

"Bravo, my young apprentices," he said, his voice dripping with theatrical flair. "You have taken your first steps into a larger world."

Daniel exchanged glances with his friends, a silent understanding passing between them. They had emerged from the echo chambers not just as survivors, but as warriors ready to take on the absurdities of their twisted reality.

And with Professor Zander as their guide, they knew that this was only the beginning of their journey to restore sanity to a world gone mad.

Suddenly, the virtual world around them glitched and distorted, a cacophony of pixels and static. A towering figure materialized before them, a grotesque amalgamation of every absurd conspiracy theory and fake news headline they had encountered. The virtual boss had arrived.

"Well, well, well," the boss sneered, its voice a grating mix of robotic glitches and human smugness. "If it isn't the little truth seekers. You think you can defeat me with your facts and logic?"

Daniel stepped forward, his virtual avatar pulsing with determination. "We've seen through your lies and deception. It's time to end this."

The boss laughed, a sound that sent shivers down their digital spines. "You fools! I am the embodiment of misinformation itself. You cannot hope to win against me."

Alice rolled her eyes. "Oh, spare us the theatrics, you overgrown glitch. We've dealt with worse than you."

The battle began, a flurry of rapid-fire arguments and razor-sharp wit. The boss hurled conspiracy theories at them, each one more outlandish than the last. But the group stood their ground, countering with facts and reason.

Kyle's fingers danced across a virtual keyboard, his tech skills put to the ultimate test as he hacked through the boss's defenses. "Guys, I think I found a weak spot! If we can expose the logical fallacies in its arguments, we might be able to take it down."

Daniel nodded, a grin spreading across his face. "Then let's hit it with everything we've got."

They launched a barrage of counterarguments, their words precise and powerful. The boss staggered under the onslaught, its form flickering and glitching.

"No!" it roared. "I will not be defeated by mere truth!"

But it was too late. With a final, devastating blow of logic, the boss shattered into a million pixels, its reign of misinformation finally at an end.

The group stood victorious, their avatars glowing with triumph. They had done it. They had proven that even in a world filled with absurdity, the truth could still prevail.

As the virtual world faded away, they found themselves back in the warehouse, their bodies drenched in sweat and their minds reeling from the intensity of the battle.

Professor Zander applauded, his eyes twinkling with pride. "Magnificent! You have shown that you have what it takes to challenge the absurdities of this world. Well done, my young rebels."

Daniel exchanged high-fives with his friends, a sense of camaraderie and purpose burning within them. They had completed their training, but he knew that this was only the beginning.

With their newfound skills and unbreakable bond, they were ready to take on anything that Brayden Funkledor's dystopian regime could throw at them. And they would do it with laughter, wit, and an unwavering commitment to the truth.

The scene ends with the group walking out of the warehouse, their heads held high and their spirits unbreakable. They had become the heroes this absurd world so desperately needed, and they were just getting started.

Professor Zander cleared his throat, drawing the group's attention. "My dear students, you have exceeded all expectations. Your ability to navigate the absurdities of this dystopian society is truly remarkable." He gestured grandly, his feathered hat wobbling precariously on his head.

Daniel grinned, still riding the high of their virtual victory. "Well, we had a pretty awesome mentor," he said, giving Professor Zander a playful wink.

"Flattery will get you everywhere, my boy," Professor Zander chuckled. His expression turned serious as he continued, "But now, it's time for you to take your skills to the real world. Use what you've learned to challenge the status quo, to bring about change in this twisted society."

Alice nodded, her eyes sparkling with determination. "We're ready, Professor. We won't let you down."

"I have no doubt about that," Professor Zander said, a smile tugging at his lips. "Remember, laughter is your weapon, and truth is your shield. Never let them break your spirit."

With those final words of wisdom, Professor Zander bowed theatrically and exited the warehouse, leaving the group to their own devices.

Kyle flopped down on a tattered couch, letting out a contented sigh. "Man, that was one hell of a training session. I feel like I could take on the world."

"Or at least Brayden Funkledor's ridiculous regime," Alice quipped, plopping down beside him.

Daniel couldn't help but laugh. "Can you imagine the look on his face when we start using his own absurd tactics against him?"

The group erupted into laughter, their spirits high and their bond stronger than ever. They spent the next hour reminiscing about their training experience, sharing inside jokes and plotting their next move.

As the laughter died down, Daniel felt a sense of purpose settle over him. They had a mission, a calling to bring about change in this dystopian world. And with his friends by his side, he knew they could accomplish anything.

"Alright, team," he said, standing up and clapping his hands together. "Let's get to work. We've got a regime to overthrow and a society to save."

The group cheered, their determination and camaraderie palpable in the air. They were ready to take on whatever challenges lay ahead, armed with their wit, their skills, and their unbreakable bond.

The chapter ended with the group marching out of the warehouse, their laughter echoing through the dilapidated streets. They were the unlikely heroes this absurd world needed, and they were damn well going to make a difference, one ridiculous encounter at a time.

The line outside the Department of Citizen Compliance stretched down the block, a serpentine mass of sweaty bodies and dour faces. Daniel shifted his weight from foot to foot, already regretting his decision to come here on his day off. His friends Alice and Kyle stood beside him, equally unenthused.

"Remind me why we're subjecting ourselves to this bullshit again?" Alice grumbled, fanning herself with a crumpled piece of paper.

Daniel sighed. "Because if we don't get our Existence Permits renewed, we'll be persona non grata in this godforsaken city."

Kyle snorted. "Right. Can't have that, can we? Might actually be an improvement."

A portly man in a rumpled suit approached the line, clutching a clipboard. His name badge read "Roger Chuddly, Assistant Deputy of Bureaucratic Efficiency."

"Attention, citizens!" Roger bellowed, his voice nasal and grating. "By order of the Department, all individuals seeking services must complete Form 1047-B before entering the building. Failure to do so will result in immediate ejection from the premises and potential fines."

He began distributing thick packets of paper to the groaning crowd. Daniel took one and flipped through it, his eyebrows climbing higher with each page.

"What the ever-loving fuck is this?" he muttered. "It's like they took every asinine question they could think of and crammed it into one form."

Alice peered over his shoulder. "Oh look, they want to know your favorite color, in case it indicates subversive tendencies."

"And your preferred brand of toilet paper," Kyle chimed in. "Vital information for the functioning of the state, obviously."

Daniel shook his head in disgust. The line inched forward at a glacial pace as people grappled with the absurd paperwork. Ahead of them, Roger paced back and forth officiously, his beady eyes scanning for any sign of noncompliance.

"I bet that clipboard is just for show," Kyle whispered. "Probably doesn't even know how to read, the stupid prick."

Alice elbowed him. "Shh, he'll hear you! Last thing we need is to get dragged off to a reeducation center for 'disrespecting an official.'"

Daniel tuned out their bickering, focusing on the form. The questions grew increasingly inane and invasive with each section. He had to resist the urge to crumple the whole thing up and shove it down Roger's throat.

This is what we've been reduced to, he thought bitterly. Jumping through hoops for a bunch of power-tripping bureaucrats, just to prove we have the right to exist. What a joke.

He scribbled nonsensical answers in the blanks, not even bothering to keep his handwriting legible. Beside him, Alice and Kyle did the same, their pens scratching furiously.

"Next!" Roger shouted, jolting Daniel from his thoughts. He realized they had reached the front of the line at last. Daniel stepped forward and slapped his completed form into Roger's outstretched hand.

Here goes nothing, he thought as Roger scrutinized the paperwork with a frown...

Roger's frown deepened as he flipped through the forms, his eyes darting from one page to another. He shuffled the papers around haphazardly, mixing up the carefully filled-out sections with careless abandon.

"Hey, watch it!" Alice hissed under her breath, her eyes widening as she watched the official create a jumbled mess of their hard work.

Daniel clenched his jaw, fighting the urge to snatch the papers back from Roger's incompetent grasp. He glanced at Kyle, who looked ready to explode with frustration.

Around them, the waiting citizens began to murmur and shift restlessly, their own forms clutched tightly in their hands. The line behind them had grown even longer, snaking around the corner and out of sight.

Roger, oblivious to the mounting tension, continued to shuffle the forms like a deck of cards. He squinted at the pages, his lips moving silently as he tried to make sense of the jumbled information.

"Uh, sir?" Daniel ventured, his voice tight with forced politeness. "Is there a problem with our forms?"

Roger looked up, blinking owlishly. "Problem? No, no problem. Just... processing."

He tapped the stack of papers against his clipboard, the sound echoing in the suddenly silent room. Then, with a shrug, he tossed the forms onto a nearby table, where they landed in a haphazard pile.

"All done!" Roger announced cheerfully, turning back to the line. "Next!"

Daniel, Alice, and Kyle exchanged incredulous looks. Their carefully filled-out forms, the key to their very existence in this twisted bureaucracy, had been carelessly discarded like yesterday's trash.

Around them, the waiting citizens erupted in a chorus of angry shouts and protests. They surged forward, waving their own forms in the air, demanding to be seen, to be heard, to be acknowledged as more than just numbers on a page.

Daniel felt a surge of anger rising in his chest. This was it, he realized. The final straw. They couldn't keep playing by these ridiculous rules, jumping through hoops for a system that didn't give a damn about them.

It was time to take a stand, to fight back against the absurdity and injustice of it all. And as he looked at Alice and Kyle, he knew they were thinking the same thing.

They exchanged a nod, a silent agreement to take action. Daniel took a deep breath, ready to confront Roger and the broken system he represented.

But before he could speak, a voice rang out from the back of the room...

Daniel whirled around, expecting to see another frustrated citizen ready to join their cause. Instead, he was met with the sight of Roger, clipboard in hand, staring at the crowd with a blank expression.

"What's the purpose of all this?" Daniel demanded, gesturing to the jumbled pile of forms on the table. "Why are we even filling out these ridiculous forms?"

Roger blinked slowly, as if processing the question. "It's necessary for efficiency," he said, his voice monotone. "The forms ensure that everything runs smoothly."

Alice scoffed. "Smoothly? You call this smoothly?" She pointed to the chaos around them, the angry faces of the waiting citizens. "This is a complete disaster!"

Roger shrugged, seemingly oblivious to the frustration mounting in the room. "The forms are essential," he repeated, like a malfunctioning robot stuck on a single line of code. "Without them, there would be no order."

Daniel shook his head in disbelief. "Order? You're creating more chaos than anything else!"

But Roger wasn't listening. He turned back to the pile of forms and began shuffling through them, mumbling to himself. "Let's see... who's next? Ah, here we go!" He pulled out a crumpled form from the middle of the stack and squinted at the name. "Bartholemew Wigglesworth? Is there a Bartholemew Wigglesworth here?"

The crowd erupted in a chorus of groans and complaints. "That's not fair!" someone shouted. "I've been waiting for hours!"

Roger ignored the protests and continued calling out random names from the jumbled stack of papers. "Gertrude Fluffybottom? Reginald Snicklefritz? Where are you?"

Daniel felt his blood boiling. This was beyond absurd. They were being subjected to the whims of a madman, a bureaucratic nightmare come to life.

He glanced at Alice and Kyle, who looked equally fuming. They had to do something, anything, to put an end to this insanity.

But what could they do? They were just three people against an entire system, a machine designed to grind them down and spit them out.

As Roger continued to call out nonsensical names, Daniel clenched his fists and tried to think. There had to be a way out of this, a way to beat the system at its own game.

And then, suddenly, an idea began to form in his mind...

Daniel leaned in close to Alice and Kyle, his eyes glinting with mischief. "I've got a plan," he whispered, his voice low and conspiratorial. "But I'm gonna need your help."

Alice raised an eyebrow, intrigued. "What did you have in mind?"

Daniel glanced around to make sure no one was listening, then spoke quickly and quietly. "I'm going to distract Roger by pretending I lost my form. While he's helping me look for it, you two swap out the jumbled stack of papers with a neatly organized one."

Kyle grinned, catching on immediately. "Brilliant. But where are we gonna get a neatly organized stack of forms?"

Daniel smirked. "Leave that to me. Just be ready to make the switch when I give the signal."

He took a deep breath, then stepped out of line and approached Roger, his face a mask of feigned concern. "Excuse me, sir? I think I may have dropped my form somewhere. Could you help me look for it?"

Roger blinked, momentarily thrown off by the request. "Uh, sure. Where did you last see it?"

"I'm not sure," Daniel said, his voice trembling with manufactured distress. "I had it when I got in line, but now it's gone. Please, you have to help me find it. I can't afford to lose my place in line."

As Roger set down the stack of forms and began to search the ground around them, Daniel caught Alice's eye and gave a subtle nod.

Moving quickly and quietly, Alice and Kyle slipped out of line and made their way to the front of the crowd. Kyle reached into his backpack and pulled out a neatly organized stack of forms, identical to the ones Roger had been holding.

With deft movements, they swapped the jumbled stack with the organized one, then melted back into the crowd before anyone noticed.

Meanwhile, Daniel continued to lead Roger on a wild goose chase, pointing to random spots on the ground and exclaiming, "I think it might have blown over there! No, wait, maybe it's under that bench!"

As the minutes ticked by, the crowd grew increasingly restless, their frustration mounting with each passing second.

Finally, after what felt like an eternity, Daniel let out a triumphant shout. "Found it! It was in my back pocket the whole time. Silly me!"

Roger straightened up, his face red and sweaty from the exertion. "Well, I'm glad you found it," he grumbled, picking up the stack of forms and shuffling back to his post.

Daniel grinned at Alice and Kyle as he slipped back into line, his eyes twinkling with barely contained laughter.

Now all they had to do was wait and see if their plan had worked...

Roger returned to his post, clutching the stack of forms tightly to his chest. He glanced down at the papers, ready to resume his haphazard name-calling, when he noticed something strange. The forms, which had been a jumbled mess just moments ago, were now perfectly organized, with each citizen's information neatly filled out and easily readable.

"What the..." Roger muttered under his breath, his brow furrowing in confusion. He flipped through the stack, double-checking that his eyes weren't playing tricks on him. But no, the forms were indeed in perfect order.

Behind him, the crowd watched with bated breath, their frustration slowly giving way to curiosity. Daniel, Alice, and Kyle exchanged subtle grins, struggling to keep their faces neutral.

Roger cleared his throat, a bead of sweat trickling down his temple. He knew he had to do something, but the sudden turn of events had thrown him off balance. With a deep breath, he turned to face the crowd, a sheepish smile on his face.

"Uh, folks," he began, his voice trembling slightly. "It seems there's been a bit of a mix-up. I apologize for any confusion or inconvenience."

The crowd murmured amongst themselves, a mixture of surprise and relief washing over them. Roger, feeling the weight of their collective gaze, straightened his posture and tried to project an air of authority.

"Right then," he said, lifting the stack of forms. "Let's get this show on the road, shall we? First up, Daniel Anderson!"

Daniel stepped forward, barely suppressing a smirk as he took his form from Roger's outstretched hand. As he passed Alice and Kyle, he whispered, "Smooth moves, guys. Didn't think you had it in you."

Alice rolled her eyes, but a smile tugged at the corners of her mouth. "Never underestimate the power of a well-organized stack of papers."

As Roger continued to call out names, the line progressed smoothly, the earlier chaos nothing more than a distant memory. Daniel, Alice, and Kyle stood together, basking in the success of their impromptu plan.

"Well, that was fun," Kyle remarked, his tone dripping with sarcasm. "Remind me to never get on your bad side, Daniel. That was some Oscar-worthy acting back there."

Daniel grinned, shrugging his shoulders. "What can I say? I've always had a flair for the dramatic."

As they neared the entrance of the government office, the trio braced themselves for whatever bureaucratic absurdities lay ahead. But for now, they savored their small victory, knowing that in this dystopian world, even the most seemingly insignificant acts of defiance could make a difference.

Daniel, Alice, and Kyle stepped into the government office, their triumphant expressions quickly morphing into ones of bewilderment. The layout of the office was a maze-like monstrosity, with corridors twisting and turning in every direction, leading to countless doors marked with cryptic symbols and nonsensical signs.

"What the actual fuck?" Daniel muttered, his eyes darting from one confusing hallway to another. "Who designed this place, M.C. Escher on acid?"

Alice snorted, her gaze fixed on a sign that read "Department of Redundancy Department." "I think we've stumbled into the ninth circle of bureaucratic hell."

Kyle, ever the pragmatist, pulled out a crumpled map from his pocket. "Okay, according to this, we need to go through the 'Corridor of Eternal Paperwork' to reach the 'Chamber of Infinite Forms.' Easy peasy, right?"

Rolling his eyes, Daniel snatched the map from Kyle's hands. "Give me that. I'm not trusting any map that looks like it was drawn by a drunk toddler."

As they navigated the labyrinthine office, they encountered a receptionist sitting behind a desk, her eyes glazed over with boredom. Daniel approached her, putting on his most charming smile. "Excuse me, miss. Could you point us in the direction of the-"

The receptionist held up a hand, cutting him off. "If you wish to proceed, a rhyming request is what you need."

Daniel blinked, his smile faltering. "I'm sorry, what?"

"To get my help, you must speak in rhyme. Otherwise, you'll be waiting until the end of time," the receptionist said, her expression deadpan.

Alice and Kyle exchanged incredulous glances behind Daniel's back, trying to stifle their laughter. Daniel, however, was not amused. "You've got to be kidding me," he grumbled under his breath.

Taking a deep breath, Daniel composed himself and tried again. "Fine. We need to find the place, where we can complete our case. A room with forms galore, please show us the door."

The receptionist nodded, a hint of a smile on her face. "Down the hall, take a right, then a left. The room you seek, of bureaucracy bereft."

As they walked away from the receptionist's desk, Kyle leaned in close to Daniel. "Impressive rhyming skills, Shakespeare. Who knew you had it in you?"

Daniel shot him a withering glare. "Shut up, Kyle. Let's just find this damn room and get out of here before I lose what's left of my sanity."

Little did they know, the challenges that awaited them in the next chapter would make the convoluted forms and rhyming receptionist seem like a walk in the park. But for now, they pressed on, determined to navigate the absurdities of this dystopian world, one ridiculous obstacle at a time.

Daniel hunched over his outdated laptop, the glow of the screen illuminating his determined face in the dingy basement room. His fingers flew across the keyboard as he navigated through a labyrinth of encrypted forums and hidden chat rooms. Bingo. He'd found her - Liz Blackwell, the infamous conspiracy debunker. Daniel smirked as he typed out a cryptic message arranging a clandestine meeting at Joe's Java Joint, the quirkiest damn coffee shop in town. With the message sent, he snapped the laptop shut. Time to take this revolution offline.

The next day, Daniel pushed open the graffiti-covered door of Joe's Java Joint, the aroma of fair-trade coffee and patchouli assaulting his nostrils. Scanning the dimly lit interior, his eyes landed on a woman in the corner, nearly hidden behind towering stacks of books and a whiteboard scrawled with red-string conspiracy webs. That had to be Liz. He wove his way through the eclectic mix of patrons - starving artists, basement dwelling hackers, and tinfoil hat enthusiasts.

"Liz Blackwell?" Daniel leaned against her table, flashing his most disarming grin. "I'm Daniel. Daniel Novak. Your partner in Brayden-busting crime."

Liz glanced up, her eyes narrowing behind wire-rimmed glasses. "Keep your voice down," she hissed, kicking out the chair across from her. "Sit."

Daniel obliged, leaning in conspiratorially. "I've heard you're the best at poking holes in Brayden's bullshit propaganda. I want in. This regime's days are numbered and I aim to be the one holding the smoking gun when it all comes crashing down."

Liz cocked an eyebrow, a hint of amusement playing at the corners of her mouth. "Bold words from a basement-dwelling keyboard warrior. What makes you think you've got what it takes to go toe-to-toe with a totalitarian madman?"

Daniel met her gaze unflinchingly, a fire burning in his eyes. "Because I've seen firsthand the insanity he's inflicting on innocent people. Because I refuse to stand by and watch as he crushes free will beneath his boot. And because, quite frankly, I've got nothing left to lose. I'm all in, Liz. Whatever it takes."

Liz leaned back, considering him for a long moment. Finally, she nodded. "Alright, Novak. You've got moxie, I'll give you that. Let's see if you can put your money where your mouth is. Welcome to the resistance."

Daniel grinned, adrenaline already pumping through his veins. Watch out, Brayden Funkledor. Your days are numbered.

Liz fixed Daniel with a piercing stare, her fingers steepled beneath her chin. "Alright, hotshot. Let's see how deep your conspiracy theory knowledge really goes. Who was behind the Great Toilet Paper Shortage of '22?"

Daniel's mind raced, his palms suddenly sweaty. "Uh, the Illuminati? No, wait! The lizard people!"

Liz snorted, shaking her head. "Wrong and wrong. It was the Chuddie Scouts, hoarding it all for their annual TP'ing of the Funkledor statue. Any self-respecting conspiracy theorist knows that."

Daniel's face flushed, but he soldiered on. "Okay, but what about the mind control chemicals in the water supply? That's gotta be Brayden's doing, right?"

"Please," Liz scoffed. "That's just a cover-up for the real truth: the government's been putting microchips in our dental fillings for years. Wake up, sheeple!"

As Daniel fumbled his way through a few more questions, his earnestness and determination shone through. Liz's skepticism slowly gave way to a grudging respect. Maybe this guy had what it took after all.

Suddenly, a voice piped up from a nearby table. "Excuse me, but did I overhear you talking about taking down Brayden Funkledor?"

Daniel and Liz whipped around to see a scrawny, bespectacled man leaning towards them, his eyes wide with excitement.

"Who's asking?" Liz demanded, her guard instantly up.

The man held up his hands in a placating gesture. "I'm Tim. I used to be a Chuddie, but I've seen the light. Brayden's nothing but a power-hungry tyrant, and I want to help bring him down."

Daniel and Liz exchanged a wary glance. Could they trust this guy? But the fire in Tim's eyes seemed genuine, and they couldn't afford to turn away potential allies.

"Alright, Tim," Daniel said slowly. "What's your story?"

As Tim launched into his tale of disillusionment and rebellion, Daniel couldn't help but feel a spark of hope. Maybe, just maybe, they stood a chance against Brayden after all. With Liz's brilliance, Tim's inside knowledge, and his own stubborn determination, anything was possible.

Watch out, Funkledor. The resistance is coming for you.

Daniel leaned back in his chair, a grin spreading across his face as Tim regaled them with stories of Brayden's ridiculous policies and the Chuddies' blind obedience. "I once saw a Chuddie cite Brayden's 'Funkledor's First Law of Fashion' to justify wearing socks with sandals," Tim snickered. "I mean, who does that?"

Liz snorted, her eyes sparkling with mirth. "That's nothing. I infiltrated one of their 'Funky Friday' meetings, and they were literally worshipping a giant statue of Brayden made entirely out of cheese."

"Cheese?" Daniel echoed, his eyebrows shooting up. "You've got to brie kidding me!"

The trio burst into laughter, their shared frustration with the absurdity of their world bringing them closer together. As their chuckles subsided, Daniel felt a warmth spreading through his chest. For the first time in years, he didn't feel alone in his fight.

"You know," Liz said thoughtfully, twirling a strand of her neon-green hair around her finger, "we can't take down Brayden alone. We need more people on our side, people who see through his bullshit and want to make a change."

Daniel nodded, his mind already whirring with possibilities. "But how do we find them? It's not like we can just put up a billboard that says 'Calling all conspiracy theorists, join the resistance today!'"

Liz's eyes suddenly lit up, a mischievous grin spreading across her face. "Why not? We might not be able to put up a billboard, but we can throw a party. A conspiracy theory-themed party, where like-minded people can come together and join our cause."

Daniel and Tim exchanged a skeptical glance. "A party?" Tim asked, his brow furrowing. "Isn't that a bit... frivolous?"

Liz leaned forward, her voice low and conspiratorial. "That's the beauty of it. Brayden and his goons will never suspect a thing. They'll just think we're a bunch of weirdos in tinfoil hats, while we're secretly building an army right under their noses."

As the idea sank in, Daniel could feel a grin tugging at the corners of his mouth. It was so crazy, it just might work. "Alright, Liz," he said, extending his hand across the table. "Let's do this. Let's throw the most epic conspiracy theory party this dystopian hellscape has ever seen."

Liz and Tim placed their hands on top of his, their faces alight with determination and just a touch of mischief. "To the resistance," Liz declared, her voice ringing with conviction.

"To the resistance," Daniel and Tim echoed, their hearts swelling with a newfound sense of purpose.

Brayden Funkledor, watch out. The rebels are coming, and they're armed with tinfoil hats and a whole lot of attitude.

Daniel, Liz, and Tim huddled around the whiteboard, their faces scrunched in concentration as they brainstormed potential venues for their conspiracy theory-themed party. Liz's marker squeaked against the board, jotting down ideas as they flew from their mouths.

"What about the abandoned warehouse on the outskirts of town?" Tim suggested, his eyes gleaming with excitement.

Liz shook her head, her curls bouncing. "Too obvious. Brayden's goons would be all over that in a heartbeat."

Daniel tapped his chin, his mind whirring. "How about the old library? It's been closed for years, but I bet we could sneak in."

Liz considered the idea for a moment before a grin spread across her face. "That's perfect! It's got that creepy, abandoned vibe that's totally on-brand for our theme."

With their venue decided, the trio set out to secure the location. But navigating the bizarre rules and regulations imposed by Brayden's government proved to be a challenge. They found themselves tangled in a web of red tape and bureaucratic nonsense.

"You need a permit to breathe in a public space," the bored-looking clerk at the government office drawled, barely glancing up from his computer screen.

Daniel leaned forward, his voice dripping with sarcasm. "Oh, I'm sorry. I didn't realize my lungs needed government approval."

The clerk merely shrugged, unimpressed by Daniel's wit. "No permit, no party. Next!"

Undeterred, the trio resorted to more creative methods. They posed as a group of eccentric librarians, convinced a janitor to lend them his keys, and even attempted to bribe a security guard with a lifetime supply of tinfoil hats.

After a series of comical misunderstandings and narrow escapes, they finally managed to secure the old library for their party. Exhausted but triumphant, they collapsed onto the dusty floor, their laughter echoing through the empty halls.

"Well, that was a wild ride," Tim remarked, wiping tears of mirth from his eyes.

Liz sat up, her face suddenly serious. "Alright, boys. We've got our venue, but now the real work begins. We need to divide and conquer if we're going to pull this off."

Daniel and Tim nodded, their expressions mirroring Liz's determination. They huddled closer, ready to hash out their respective roles.

"Daniel, you're in charge of spreading the word," Liz declared, her finger jabbing in his direction. "Use your charm and wit to create a buzz. Make people curious, but don't give away too much."

Daniel grinned, his eyes sparkling with mischief. "Leave it to me. I'll have them eating out of the palm of my hand."

Liz turned to Tim, her voice firm. "Tim, you handle the logistics and catering. We need to keep our guests fed and watered, but more importantly, we need to keep them focused on the cause."

Tim saluted, his face a mask of mock solemnity. "Aye aye, captain. I'll make sure the only thing they're hungry for is revolution."

"And I," Liz continued, a sly smile playing on her lips, "will focus on the decorations. I've got some ideas for hidden messages and symbols that will speak to our fellow rebels."

As they set about their tasks, a sense of camaraderie and purpose settled over the trio. They were no longer just three misfits in a world gone mad. They were the spark of a revolution, and they were ready to ignite the flames of change.

Daniel, armed with his infectious enthusiasm and quick wit, ventured out into the streets of the dystopian city, determined to rally support for their cause. He approached a group of street performers, their vibrant costumes and exaggerated movements a stark contrast to the drab surroundings.

"Hey there, my fellow artistes!" Daniel called out, his voice carrying over the din of the crowd. "How would you like to be part of something extraordinary?"

The performers eyed him suspiciously, their painted faces contorted in confusion. "What's in it for us?" a lanky juggler asked, his voice laced with skepticism.

Daniel leaned in conspiratorially, his eyes twinkling with mischief. "Picture this: a gathering of like-minded individuals, all united in the pursuit of truth and justice. A chance to stick it to the man and have a damn good time doing it."

The performers exchanged glances, their curiosity piqued. "Tell us more," a fire-breather demanded, her voice raspy from years of breathing flames.

Daniel launched into a passionate speech, his words painting a picture of a world where creativity and individuality reigned supreme. He spoke of the absurdity of the government's rules and regulations, of the need for change and the power of unity.

As he spoke, the performers' eyes widened, their initial skepticism replaced by a growing sense of excitement. They nodded along, their faces split into wide grins as they envisioned the possibilities.

"Count us in," the juggler declared, his voice filled with newfound determination. "We'll be there, and we'll bring our A-game."

Daniel clapped him on the back, his own face mirroring their enthusiasm. "Excellent! Spread the word, but remember, this is an underground operation. We can't let the Chuddies catch wind of our plans."

With a final wink and a conspiratorial nod, Daniel bid the performers farewell, his heart swelling with pride at the small victory. He continued his mission, approaching other eccentric characters throughout the city, his charm and wit winning them over one by one.

Meanwhile, Liz had transformed their makeshift headquarters into a visual spectacle, her conspiracy theory-themed decorations filling every available surface. She had spent hours poring over ancient texts and obscure websites, gleaning hidden messages and symbols that she wove into the fabric of her creations.

Giant posters adorned the walls, their surfaces covered in cryptic codes and enigmatic imagery. Strings of lights hung from the ceiling, their colors pulsing in a hypnotic rhythm that seemed to whisper secrets to those who knew how to listen.

As Daniel and Tim returned from their respective tasks, they stopped short, their jaws dropping at the sight before them. Liz stood in the center of the room, a triumphant grin on her face as she surveyed her handiwork.

"Holy shit, Liz," Daniel breathed, his eyes wide with amazement. "This is incredible."

Tim nodded in agreement, his own face split into a grin. "I feel like I've stepped into a fevered dream, but in the best possible way."

Liz beamed, her chest swelling with pride. "This is just the beginning, boys. Wait until our guests see what we've got in store for them."

The trio shared a laugh, their voices echoing through the transformed space. They moved closer, their arms wrapping around each other in a fierce embrace. In that moment, they knew that they were more than just a ragtag group of misfits. They were a family, bound by a shared purpose and an unbreakable bond.

As they pulled away, their eyes shining with a mix of excitement and determination, they knew that the real work was just beginning. But for now, they allowed themselves a moment to bask in the glow of their achievements, secure in the knowledge that they were one step closer to bringing about the change they so desperately sought.

The clock ticked closer to the party's start time, and Daniel, Liz, and Tim found themselves pacing the room, their nerves fraying with each passing minute. The decorations loomed around them, a testament to their hard work and dedication, but doubt began to creep in, insidious and unrelenting.

"What if no one shows up?" Tim whispered, his voice barely audible over the hum of the fluorescent lights.

Liz shook her head, her lips pressed into a thin line. "They'll come. They have to."

Daniel ran a hand through his hair, his eyes darting to the door. "Maybe we're fooling ourselves. Maybe we're just a bunch of delusional misfits tilting at windmills."

The words hung heavy in the air, a suffocating blanket of uncertainty. They looked at each other, their faces etched with a mix of fear and desperation. The clock ticked on, a mocking reminder of their dwindling hope.

Just as they were about to succumb to their doubts, the door burst open, and a figure stepped inside, clad head to toe in a shimmering aluminum foil suit. "Greetings, fellow truth-seekers!" the figure proclaimed, striking a dramatic pose.

Daniel, Liz, and Tim stared in disbelief, their mouths agape. The figure strode forward, extending a hand wrapped in foil. "I'm here for the party. I hope I'm not too early."

Laughter bubbled up from deep within them, a release of tension and a spark of renewed hope. "Not at all," Liz grinned, grasping the offered hand. "Welcome to the resistance."

As if on cue, more guests began to arrive, each one dressed in a more outlandish costume than the last. A woman wearing a hat made entirely of newspaper clippings, a man in a suit covered in blurry photographs of UFOs, a group of friends dressed as the different branches of the Illuminati.

The room quickly filled with a cacophony of laughter and chatter, the guests mingling and admiring each other's costumes. Daniel, Liz, and Tim moved through the crowd, their earlier doubts forgotten as they basked in the energy of their newfound allies.

"Can you believe this turnout?" Tim marveled, his eyes shining with excitement.

Daniel nodded, a grin spreading across his face. "It's like we've tapped into something bigger than ourselves. Like we're part of a movement."

Liz raised her glass, her voice ringing out above the din. "To the resistance!" she cried, her words met with a resounding cheer.

As the party raged on, Daniel, Liz, and Tim knew that they had taken the first step towards something extraordinary. They had found their people, their tribe, and together, they would fight against the absurdity of their world, one conspiracy theory at a time.

Daniel, Liz, and Tim stood on a makeshift stage, their faces flushed with triumph and a hint of disbelief. The room buzzed with the electric energy of their newfound allies, each person united by a shared desire to challenge the dystopian absurdity that had consumed their lives.

"This is incredible," Daniel whispered, his eyes scanning the crowd. "I never imagined we'd find so many people who feel the same way we do."

Liz nodded, a mischievous glint in her eye. "And to think, it all started with a few conspiracy theories and a whiteboard."

Tim chuckled, raising his glass. "To the power of unlikely alliances and even more unlikely decorations!"

As they clinked their glasses together, a hush fell over the room. Daniel stepped forward, his voice carrying a newfound confidence. "Friends, fellow truth-seekers, and rebels against the nonsensical," he began, "we stand here today not as individuals, but as a united front. A force to be reckoned with in the face of Brayden Funkledor's ridiculous regime."

The crowd erupted in cheers and applause, their faces alight with a shared sense of purpose. Liz and Tim exchanged a look of pride, their hearts swelling with the realization that they had played a part in bringing this moment to fruition.

"But this is only the beginning," Daniel continued, his tone growing more serious. "We have a long road ahead of us, filled with challenges, setbacks, and undoubtedly more absurdity than we can possibly imagine. But together, armed with our wits, our determination, and our unwavering commitment to the truth, we will prevail."

As the crowd roared their approval, Daniel, Liz, and Tim raised their glasses once more, their eyes locked in a silent promise. They knew that the path before them would be far from easy, but with their quirky and determined allies by their side, they were ready to take on whatever lay ahead.

The chapter drew to a close, the air crackling with the energy of a revolution on the brink of ignition. Daniel, Liz, and Tim stood tall, their hearts full of hope and their minds racing with the possibilities of what the future might hold. Together, they would fight, they would laugh, and they would expose the truth, one ridiculous conspiracy at a time.

Daniel, Alice, Kyle, and their friends trudged down the crowded city street, jostling for space amidst a sea of bizarrely attired citizens. A corpulent man squeezed past them wearing a neon green unitard emblazoned with Brayden Funkledor's leering face. Alice snorted. "Nice outfit, buddy."

The man glared at her. "It's the official Brayden Funkledor Fan Club uniform, you cretin! Only the most loyal supporters get to wear these."

"Lucky us," muttered Daniel under his breath. He craned his neck, peering past the throngs of people at the gargantuan billboards towering above. Each one depicted a different heroic pose of their fearless leader — Brayden riding a bald eagle, Brayden flexing his flabby biceps, Brayden french-kissing an American flag. It was enough to make Daniel want to puke his guts out.

Kyle nudged him. "Check it out, man. Looks like some kind of batshit rally going on up ahead."

Daniel followed his gaze to the town square, where a massive crowd had gathered, waving oversized foam fingers with Brayden's face plastered on them. A booming voice erupted from the loudspeakers:

"WHO DO WE LOVE?"

"BRAYDEN FUNKLEDOR!" the crowd chanted back in cultish unison.

"I CAN'T HEAR YOU!"

"BRAYDEN FUNKLEDOR!!!"

The chanting swelled to a deafening roar. Daniel exchanged an incredulous look with Alice. This was some next-level brainwashing bullshit. As they approached the fringes of the rally, a chipper woman in a star-spangled pantsuit thrust foam fingers into their hands.

"Welcome, patriots! Join us in pledging your undying allegiance to our Supreme Leader!"

"Uh, thanks but no thanks, Lady Liberty," Alice said, subtly flipping her the bird. "We were just passing through."

The woman's smile tightened. "Attendance is mandatory, sweetie. Now put those fingers on and start chanting before the Absurdity Patrol notices. And make it snappy!"

She shoved the foam abominations at them again, eyes darting to the hulking officers in ridiculous getups patrolling the perimeter. Daniel glanced at his friends. With resignation, they each took a finger.

Fuck it, he thought. When in dystopia, do as the dystopians do. He slipped the monstrosity onto his hand and halfheartedly pumped it in the air.

"Brayden Funkledor, Brayden Funkledor," he chanted without enthusiasm.

Alice shot him the stink eye but joined in, as did Kyle and the others. They obediently parroted the insipid slogans as the rally reached a fever pitch around them, each secretly wondering how in the hell their once-sane society had devolved into this bizarre nightmare.

As they shuffled through the crowd, trying to keep a low profile, Daniel noticed an elderly woman being accosted by two officers from the Absurdity Patrol. The poor woman was wearing mismatched socks—one striped, one polka-dotted—and the officers were having none of it.

"Ma'am, are you aware that mismatched socks are a violation of the Fashion Conformity Act?" the taller officer barked, his face contorted into an exaggerated scowl beneath his comically oversized hat.

The woman looked bewildered. "But I've been wearing mismatched socks for years! It's my signature style!"

"Not anymore, it isn't," the shorter officer sneered, whipping out a notepad. "That's a fifty-dollar fine and a mandatory fashion re-education class for you, missy."

Daniel couldn't believe what he was witnessing. He leaned over to Alice and whispered, "Is this seriously happening right now?"

Alice rolled her eyes. "Welcome to the new normal, where fashion crimes are apparently a thing."

Suddenly, the crowd around them began to shift and sway. A beat pulsed through the air, and Daniel realized with growing dread that one of Brayden's campaign jingles was blasting from the loudspeakers.

"Oh no," Kyle groaned. "Not the dance routine. Anything but the dance routine."

But it was too late. The citizens around them had already begun to move in eerie synchronization, their limbs jerking and flailing in a bizarre parody of a flash mob. Daniel and his friends stood frozen, unsure of what to do.

"Blend in," Alice hissed through clenched teeth. "We can't draw attention to ourselves."

Reluctantly, they began to mimic the movements of the crowd, their faces twisted into grimaces of discomfort and embarrassment. Daniel felt like a complete idiot as he shuffled his feet and waved his foam finger in time with the music.

This is insane, he thought, catching Kyle's eye and sharing a look of commiseration. *We've got to find a way to put an end to this madness before it's too late.*

As the dance routine reached its cringe-worthy crescendo, Daniel's mind raced with possibilities. There had to be a way to break free from this absurdity and restore some semblance of sanity to their world. But first, they had to survive this flash mob from hell and slip away unnoticed.

Just keep dancing, he told himself, gritting his teeth as he shimmied and shook. *Keep dancing and plot your next move. We'll find a way out of this dystopian nightmare, one ridiculous step at a time.*

Daniel and his friends managed to slip away from the flash mob, their faces flushed with a mixture of relief and embarrassment. As they hurried down the street, desperate to put some distance between themselves and the unsettling display of synchronized absurdity, they stumbled upon a government building.

"Oh great, what fresh hell awaits us here?" Kyle muttered, eyeing the imposing structure with suspicion.

A steady stream of frustrated citizens poured out of the building, their faces contorted with anger and disbelief. Curious, Daniel approached a middle-aged woman who was clutching a loaf of bread as if it were a hard-won trophy.

"Excuse me, ma'am," he said, putting on his most charming smile. "What's going on in there?"

The woman let out a humorless laugh. "If you want to buy a loaf of bread, you've got to fill out a million forms first. Name, address, social security number, favorite color, preferred brand of toilet paper... it's ridiculous!"

Alice raised an eyebrow. "Seriously? All that just for bread?"

"Welcome to Brayden's America," the woman sighed, shaking her head. "Bureaucracy at its finest."

Intrigued, the group made their way inside the building. The scene that greeted them was one of utter chaos. Citizens stood in long, winding lines, their arms laden with stacks of paperwork. Harried bureaucrats sat behind desks, stamping forms and barking orders at the hapless citizens.

"This is insane," Daniel muttered, watching as a man argued with a particularly surly official.

"I've filled out these forms three times already!" the man shouted, waving a stack of papers in the air. "What more do you want from me?"

The official regarded him with a bored expression. "Sir, I'm afraid you'll have to fill them out again. You used blue ink instead of black. Rules are rules."

As the man sputtered with rage, Daniel and his friends exchanged incredulous looks. *How had their world come to this?*

Suddenly, a commotion erupted near the entrance of the building. A figure dressed in a giant potato costume burst through the doors, waving a stack of leaflets in the air.

"Behold!" the potato prophet cried, his voice muffled by the thick fabric of his costume. "I bring tidings from our great leader, Brayden Funkledor himself!"

The group watched in amazement as the potato prophet began to distribute the leaflets to the bewildered citizens. "Brayden has seen the future!" he declared, his eyes shining with fervor. "A future where all citizens are required to wear mismatched socks on Tuesdays and eat nothing but green jello on Thursdays!"

Daniel snatched a leaflet from the prophet's hand and scanned it quickly. The prophecies were written in a strange, cryptic language that seemed to be a mixture of English, pig Latin, and complete gibberish.

"What the hell does this even mean?" he muttered, squinting at the nonsensical words.

The potato prophet overheard him and fixed him with a stern glare. "The meanings will be revealed in time, my child. Trust in Brayden, for he knows all."

Alice snorted. "Yeah, right. Brayden couldn't find his own ass with both hands and a flashlight."

The prophet gasped, clutching at his chest as if he'd been struck. "Blasphemy!" he cried, pointing a finger at Alice. "You dare to speak ill of our glorious leader?"

As the prophet continued to rant and rave, spouting increasingly bizarre prophecies and warnings of doom, Daniel and his friends slowly backed away. *This was getting way too weird, even for them.*

"Let's get out of here," Kyle muttered, eyeing the prophet warily. "Before he starts demanding sacrifices or something."

The group nodded in agreement and made a hasty retreat, leaving the government building and its strange inhabitants behind. As they emerged onto the street, blinking in the harsh sunlight, Daniel couldn't help but feel a sense of despair wash over him.

Was this really what their world had come to? A place where even the simplest tasks were mired in bureaucracy and absurdity? Where potato prophets roamed the streets, spouting nonsense and worshipping a madman?

He shook his head, trying to clear his thoughts. No, he couldn't give up hope. Not yet. There had to be a way to fight back against this insanity, to restore some semblance of normalcy to their lives.

Daniel looked at his friends, seeing the same determination etched on their faces. They were in this together, no matter what. And together, they would find a way to bring Brayden Funkledor's reign of absurdity to an end.

One ridiculous obstacle at a time.

As they walked further into the city, Daniel and his friends stumbled upon a park bustling with activity. People were gathered in small groups, huddled over what appeared to be bingo cards. Curiosity piqued, they approached a nearby group to get a better look.

"B-3, combover!" a middle-aged woman shouted, her eyes darting around the park.

"What the hell?" Alice muttered, her brow furrowed in confusion.

A man beside the woman suddenly jumped up, his hand shooting into the air. "Bingo! I got it! Oversized tie, combover, and the signature smirk!"

Daniel watched in disbelief as the man proudly displayed his bingo card, which was filled with various physical attributes of Brayden Funkledor. *Was this really what passed for entertainment these days?*

"Step right up, folks!" a voice boomed from nearby. "Get your Brayden Bingo cards here! Spot the Supreme Leader's glorious features and win fabulous prizes!"

The group exchanged glances, torn between amusement and disgust. Kyle, however, seemed intrigued.

"You know what? I'm gonna play," he declared, fishing in his pocket for some cash.

"Are you serious?" Daniel asked, his eyebrows shooting up.

"Why not?" Kyle shrugged. "When in Rome, right?"

He strode over to the bingo card vendor, leaving his friends to watch in bewilderment. A few minutes later, he returned, clutching a bingo card and a dauber.

"Alright, let's do this," he said, his eyes scanning the park. "I'm gonna spot that combover if it's the last thing I do."

Alice rolled her eyes. "This is insane. We should be focusing on how to take Brayden down, not playing some stupid game."

Daniel nodded in agreement, but he couldn't help but feel a twinge of amusement at Kyle's enthusiasm. *Maybe a little levity was what they needed right now, even if it came in the form of a bizarre bingo game.*

As they continued through the park, they found themselves engulfed in a sea of Brayden Bingo players, all eagerly searching for the

Supreme Leader's distinctive features. Shouts of "Bingo!" rang out every few minutes, followed by cheers and groans of disappointment.

"This is surreal," Daniel muttered, shaking his head. *How had their world become so twisted, so absurd?*

Just as he was about to suggest they move on, a vendor caught his eye. The man was hawking an array of bizarre products, from "Truth Serum Lollipops" to "Conspiracy Theory T-Shirts." Daniel couldn't resist the urge to take a closer look.

"Ah, I see you're interested in my wares!" the vendor said, his eyes gleaming. "These truth serum lollipops are guaranteed to make anyone spill their deepest, darkest secrets. Perfect for interrogations or just a fun party game!"

Alice snorted. "Yeah, right. And I suppose those t-shirts will make us invisible to the government's surveillance drones?"

The vendor grinned. "You catch on quick, missy. But wait, there's more! For a limited time, I'll throw in a tin foil hat absolutely free with every purchase. You can't put a price on protecting your thoughts from mind control!"

Daniel and his friends couldn't help but laugh at the vendor's outrageous sales pitch. It was clear that he was just trying to make a quick buck off the gullible and paranoid.

"Thanks, but no thanks," Daniel said, holding up his hand. "We're not interested in your snake oil."

The vendor's smile faltered for a moment, but he quickly recovered. "Suit yourself, kid. But don't come crying to me when the government starts reading your thoughts and controlling your actions."

As they walked away, Kyle couldn't resist a parting shot. "I think I'll take my chances with the mind control. It's gotta be better than listening to your bullshit."

The vendor's indignant sputtering faded into the distance as they left the park behind, their spirits slightly lifted by the brief moment of levity. But Daniel knew that the road ahead would be far from easy. They had to stay focused on their goal, no matter how many distractions and absurdities they encountered along the way.

The fight against Brayden Funkledor was far from over, and they couldn't afford to let their guard down for even a moment.

As they turned the corner, Daniel and his friends stumbled upon a street performance that had gathered quite a crowd. A group of actors, dressed in exaggerated caricatures of Brayden Funkledor, were reenacting one of his infamous campaign speeches. The lead actor, sporting a ridiculously oversized combover and a garish red tie, gestured wildly as he delivered lines in a pitch-perfect imitation of Brayden's nasally drawl.

"We're gonna build a wall, folks! A tremendous wall! And who's gonna pay for it? The Mexicans, that's who!" the actor bellowed, eliciting a roar of laughter from the audience.

Daniel couldn't help but chuckle at the absurdity of it all. The actors were laying it on thick, but their portrayal of Brayden was spot-on. The way they captured his mannerisms, his catchphrases, his complete lack of self-awareness - it was almost too real.

But that's the problem, isn't it? Daniel thought to himself. *It's all too real. This clown is actually running the country, and people are eating it up like it's the greatest show on earth.*

As the performance went on, the actors grew more and more outlandish in their depiction of Brayden. They had him signing executive orders with a giant crayon, throwing temper tantrums on stage, and even breaking into a bizarre dance routine set to a remix of his campaign theme song.

The crowd was in stitches, but Daniel couldn't shake the feeling of unease that had settled in the pit of his stomach. *How did we let it get this far?* he wondered. *How did we let this man, this walking caricature, take control of our lives?*

Lost in thought, Daniel almost didn't notice when his friends started moving again. They had to keep going, had to keep searching for a way to bring Brayden down. But as they walked away from the street performance, Daniel couldn't help but feel a sense of hopelessness wash over him.

If people can laugh at this, if they can treat it like just another joke, then what chance do we really have of changing things?

But he knew he couldn't afford to think like that. They had to keep fighting, no matter how bleak things seemed. And so, with a heavy heart and a determined stride, Daniel pressed on into the heart of the city, ready to face whatever fresh absurdities lay ahead.

As they continued their journey, the group came across a government-sponsored art installation that stopped them dead in their tracks. In the middle of a bustling square stood a colossal sculpture made entirely out of discarded fast-food wrappers, towering over the surrounding buildings like a greasy, crumpled colossus.

"What the actual fuck?" Alice muttered, her eyes wide with disbelief.

Daniel couldn't help but agree with her sentiment. The sculpture was a monstrosity, a testament to the wastefulness and excess of their society. It was as if someone had taken all the garbage from a hundred fast-food joints and mashed it together into a vaguely humanoid shape, complete with a giant, grinning head that bore an unsettling resemblance to Brayden Funkledor himself.

"I don't even know what to say," Kyle said, shaking his head. "Is this supposed to be art? Or some kind of sick joke?"

"Knowing our government, probably both," Alice replied, her voice dripping with sarcasm.

As they stood there, marveling at the sheer absurdity of the sculpture, Daniel couldn't help but feel a sense of anger rising up inside him. *This is what our tax dollars are going towards?* he thought bitterly. *Giant piles of trash masquerading as art, while people are struggling just to put food on the table?*

It was a stark reminder of just how far their society had fallen, of how little the powers that be cared about the well-being of their citizens. And yet, even in the face of such blatant wastefulness, people still went about their lives as if everything was normal, as if giant fast-food sculptures were just another part of the daily grind.

We have to do something, Daniel thought, his fists clenching at his sides. *We can't just sit back and let this madness continue. We have to fight back, before it's too late.*

But as he looked around at the crowds of people milling about the square, going about their business as if nothing was amiss, he couldn't help but wonder if it was already too late. If they were just too far gone, too complacent in their own destruction, to ever truly break free from the absurdity that had consumed their world.

No, he told himself firmly, shaking off the doubts that threatened to creep in. *We can't give up. We have to keep fighting, no matter what. For ourselves, for each other, for the future we know is still possible.*

And with that thought burning bright in his mind, Daniel turned to his friends, a fierce determination etched across his face.

"Come on," he said, his voice low and urgent. "We've got work to do."

As they rounded the corner, Daniel and his friends stumbled upon a sight that stopped them dead in their tracks. A group of citizens, dressed head to toe in giant pencil costumes, were marching down the street, their signs held high and their voices ringing out in a passionate chant.

"Education, not indoctrination!" they shouted, their words echoing off the buildings around them. "Critical thinking, not blind obedience!"

Daniel felt a grin spreading across his face as he watched the protest unfold. It was a rare sight these days, to see people standing up for something they believed in, something that actually mattered.

"We have to join them," he said, turning to his friends with a mischievous glint in his eye. "Come on, let's show these pencil-pushers some support."

Without waiting for a response, he darted forward, snatching up a discarded sign and hoisting it above his head. "Down with Funkledor's funky lies!" he yelled, his voice joining the chorus of chants.

Alice and Kyle exchanged a look of amusement before shrugging and joining in, their own signs held high as they marched alongside the giant pencils. For a moment, as they chanted and waved their signs, Daniel felt a sense of camaraderie, a sense of purpose that had been sorely lacking in his life.

But as they turned down another street, the mood quickly shifted. The houses here were a riot of color, each one painted in a garish shade of neon that assaulted the eyes. And everywhere they looked, there were statues of Brayden Funkledor, his smirking face leering down at them from every angle.

"What the hell is this place?" Alice muttered, her nose wrinkling in disgust as she took in the tacky decorations.

"Funkledor's Folly, by the looks of it," Kyle quipped, his voice dripping with sarcasm. "I guess when you're a megalomaniacal dictator, subtlety isn't really your strong suit."

Daniel shook his head, a wave of anger washing over him as he stared at the oversized statues. It was just another reminder of how far their society had fallen, how much power Funkledor had managed to accumulate through his lies and manipulation.

We can't let him win, he thought, his jaw clenching with determination. *We have to find a way to stop him, to bring this whole rotten system crashing down.*

But as they navigated the maze-like streets, the statues seeming to loom larger with every turn, Daniel couldn't shake the feeling that they were in over their heads. That maybe, just maybe, Funkledor's grip on power was too strong to ever truly be broken.

No, he told himself firmly, pushing the doubts aside. *We can't give up. We have to keep fighting, no matter what. For the sake of everyone who's counting on us.*

And so, with a deep breath and a renewed sense of purpose, Daniel pressed on, his friends by his side as they delved deeper into the heart of Funkledor's twisted empire.

As they turned a corner, Daniel and his friends found themselves in the midst of a heated street debate. Two passionate citizens, a man with a disheveled combover and a woman wearing a t-shirt emblazoned with Brayden's face, were locked in a shouting match.

"Brayden's policies are the best thing that's ever happened to this country!" the man bellowed, his face turning an alarming shade of red. "He's making America great again!"

"Are you kidding me?" the woman retorted, her eyes wide with disbelief. "His policies are a joke! He's running this country into the ground!"

Daniel and his friends watched in morbid fascination as the debate devolved into a flurry of nonsensical arguments and personal attacks.

"Oh yeah? Well, at least Brayden has better hair than you!" the man shouted, pointing an accusing finger at the woman's frizzy locks.

"What does that have to do with anything?" the woman screeched, throwing her hands up in exasperation.

This is insane, Daniel thought, shaking his head in disbelief. *How can anyone take this seriously?*

But as he looked around at the gathered crowd, he saw that many of them were nodding along with the man's ridiculous arguments, their faces contorted with blind loyalty to Brayden.

They're all brainwashed, he realized, a sinking feeling in his gut. *Brayden's got them so twisted up, they can't even see how absurd this all is.*

Just as the debate reached a fever pitch, a loud announcement boomed over a nearby loudspeaker.

"Attention all citizens! It's time for your mandatory fun at Brayden's Amusement Park! Please proceed to the entrance immediately!"

Daniel and his friends exchanged wary glances as the crowd began to disperse, the debate forgotten in the face of Brayden's latest decree.

"I guess we don't have much of a choice," Alice sighed, gesturing towards the towering roller coasters in the distance. "Let's just get this over with."

Reluctantly, they made their way to the amusement park entrance, where a bored-looking attendant handed them each a map.

"Welcome to Brayden's Amusement Park," he droned, his voice devoid of any enthusiasm. "Please enjoy your mandatory fun on our signature roller coasters, including the 'Make America Great Again' and the 'Build the Wall' rides."

You've got to be kidding me, Daniel thought, staring at the map in disbelief. *He's even managed to ruin amusement parks.*

But as they made their way into the park, he couldn't help but feel a flicker of excitement at the thought of riding the coasters. It had been so long since they'd had any kind of fun, any kind of escape from the constant absurdity of their lives.

Maybe this won't be so bad, he thought, a reluctant grin spreading across his face as they approached the "Make America Great Again" coaster. *At least we'll get a good adrenaline rush out of it.*

As they climbed into the coaster car and pulled down the safety bars, Daniel felt a rush of exhilaration mixed with a sense of absurdity. The coaster car was emblazoned with Brayden's face, his beady eyes staring out at them from every angle.

Here we go, he thought, bracing himself as the coaster began to climb the first hill. *Into the belly of the beast.*

And as they plunged down the first drop, screaming and laughing in equal measure, Daniel couldn't help but feel a sense of camaraderie with his friends. They were in this together, no matter how absurd things got.

We'll make it through this, he thought, as the coaster twisted and turned, Brayden's face grinning maniacally at them from every direction. *We have to.*

As they stumbled out of the amusement park, still reeling from the dizzying rides and the bombardment of Brayden's image, Daniel and his friends found themselves drawn to a commotion down the street. A crowd had gathered around a makeshift stage, where a group of street performers were setting up for what appeared to be a play.

"Oh, this oughta be good," Kyle smirked, nudging Daniel with his elbow. "Another dose of Brayden worship, I'm sure."

But as they approached the stage, it became clear that this was no ordinary performance. The actors were dressed in outlandish costumes, their faces painted with exaggerated expressions of mockery and disdain. And at the center of the stage stood a figure dressed in a suit that was a little too tight, with a wig that was a little too orange, and a tie that was a little too long.

"Is that...?" Alice trailed off, her eyes widening in disbelief.

"Brayden Funkledor," Daniel finished, a grin spreading across his face. "Or at least, a pretty damn good impression of him."

As the play began, it became clear that this was no celebration of Brayden's presidency. The actors launched into a biting satire, skewering everything from Brayden's nonsensical policies to his bizarre behavior. The dialogue was sharp and witty, filled with clever wordplay and biting sarcasm.

"My fellow Americans," the actor playing Brayden bellowed, his voice a perfect imitation of the real thing. "I stand before you today to announce my latest initiative: the 'Make America Absurd Again' campaign!"

The crowd roared with laughter, and Daniel found himself joining in. It felt good to laugh, to let loose and forget about the constant stress and fear that had become a part of their daily lives.

As the play went on, the satire only grew more pointed. The actors took aim at Brayden's cabinet, portraying them as a group of bumbling idiots who couldn't find their way out of a paper bag. They mocked Brayden's obsession with his own image, showing him constantly primping and preening in front of a mirror.

This is brilliant, Daniel thought, wiping tears of laughter from his eyes. *Finally, someone is saying what we're all thinking.*

But as the play reached its climax, the tone shifted. The actors dropped their comedic personas, and their faces grew serious. They spoke of the dangers of blind allegiance, of the importance of questioning authority and standing up for what was right.

"We cannot let this absurdity become our new normal," the actor playing Brayden said, his voice ringing out over the suddenly silent crowd. "We must resist, we must fight back, we must hold onto our humanity in the face of all this madness."

Daniel felt a lump forming in his throat, and he swallowed hard. He looked around at his friends, seeing the same emotion reflected in their eyes. They had been through so much together, had seen so much absurdity and chaos. But in that moment, standing there in the middle of the street, watching a group of brave performers speak truth to power, he felt a flicker of hope.

Maybe we can do this, he thought, his hands clenching into fists at his sides. *Maybe we can fight back, and maybe, just maybe, we can win.*

As the play ended and the crowd began to disperse, Daniel turned to his friends, a determined look on his face.

"Come on," he said, his voice steady and strong. "We've got work to do."

Daniel hunched over the stack of newspapers, squinting in the dim light of the musty room. The single bare bulb dangling from the ceiling cast eerie shadows across the yellowed pages. His fingers were stained with ink as he frantically flipped through the papers, searching for any scrap of truth hidden amidst the propaganda and bullshit.

"C'mon, c'mon," he muttered under his breath. "There's gotta be something here. Some clue about how we ended up with these incompetent jackasses running the show."

Page after page of mind-numbing drivel passed before his eyes. Stories about the glorious achievements of the regime, the unparalleled wisdom of the Supreme Leader, the unending prosperity enjoyed by the citizens. It was all such obvious horseshit.

Daniel was about to toss aside another useless rag when a headline caught his eye:

"Brayden Funkledor: From Reality TV Star to President-Dictator"

"What the fuck?" Daniel gasped. He blinked hard, thinking his eyes must be playing tricks in the low light. But no, there it was, printed in bold letters above a grainy photo of that moron Brayden, grinning like the village idiot.

Daniel's hands shook slightly as he lifted the paper closer to examine the article. This was the TRUTH he'd been seeking, the ugly reality behind the rise of that buffoonish tyrant. His heart pounded in his ears as his eyes darted over the text, hardly believing the words in front of him...

Daniel's mind reeled as he absorbed the absurd details laid out in black and white. Brayden Funkledor, the bumbling oaf who could barely string together a coherent sentence, had somehow managed to fail his way upwards from D-list celebrity to the highest office in the land.

The article painted a picture of a man with the intellect of a third-grader, a clown who had stumbled ass-backwards into power on a wave of manufactured outrage and lowest-common-denominator appeal.

Memories of Brayden's cartoonish persona on that godforsaken reality show flashed through Daniel's mind - the pratfalls, the temper tantrums, the inane catchphrases that had somehow become the rallying cries of a nation.

"Jesus Christ," Daniel muttered, his voice tinged with equal parts disbelief and disgust. "We're living in a fucking circus. A bad joke that just keeps going."

He could feel his pulse quickening, a sense of righteous anger rising in his gut. This was beyond incompetence, beyond mere idiocy. This was a perversion of everything that society was supposed to stand for, a complete inversion of logic and reason.

Daniel slammed the newspaper shut, the pages crumpling under the force of his grip. He couldn't just sit on this bombshell, couldn't let this revelation fester in the shadows. The people needed to know the truth about the clown who had seized the reins of power.

With a newfound sense of determination, Daniel sprang to his feet, the chair clattering behind him. He had to find Alice and Kyle, had to share this earth-shattering discovery with the only two people he could trust in this mad, mad world.

As he rushed out of the room, the newspaper clutched tightly in his hand, Daniel's mind was already racing ahead, plotting his next move. One way or another, he was going to expose Brayden for the fraud he was - and maybe, just maybe, strike a blow against the absurdity that had engulfed their once-sane society.

Daniel burst through the door of Alice's apartment, the newspaper still clutched in his white-knuckled grip. The dimly lit room was illuminated by the glow of multiple computer screens, casting an eerie blue hue across the cluttered space.

Alice sat hunched over her keyboard, her fingers flying across the keys as she engaged in a heated debate on a conspiracy theory forum. The rapid-fire clacking of the keyboard filled the air, punctuated by the occasional muttered curse.

"Alice, you're not gonna believe this shit," Daniel blurted out, ignoring her startled yelp as he crossed the room in a few quick strides.

"What the fuck, Daniel?" Alice snapped, whirling around in her chair to face him. "Can't you see I'm in the middle of something important here?"

But Daniel was already shoving the newspaper in her face, jabbing his finger at the headline. "Forget your goddamn forum for a second and read this. Brayden Funkledor, the fucking President-Dictator, is a reality TV star with a third-grade reading level."

Alice's eyes widened as she scanned the article, her mouth falling open in disbelief. "No fucking way," she breathed, her gaze darting back and forth across the page. "This can't be real."

"Oh, it's real alright," Daniel said grimly, his jaw clenched tight. "We've been living under the rule of a goddamn cartoon character."

As the gravity of the situation sank in, Alice's fingers froze on the keyboard, the cursor blinking accusingly on the screen. The absurdity of it all hit her like a punch to the gut, a sickening realization that their world had been turned upside down by a buffoon in a suit.

"We can't let this stand," she said slowly, her voice hardening with determination. "We have to do something, expose this clown for what he really is."

Daniel nodded, a fierce glint in his eye. "Exactly what I was thinking. We need to find Kyle and come up with a plan. This ends now."

With a decisive click, Alice closed the conspiracy theory forum, her priorities suddenly crystal clear. She stood up, grabbing her jacket from the back of the chair.

"Let's go," she said, her voice thrumming with a newfound sense of purpose. "Time to take down this circus act once and for all."

As they headed out into the chaotic streets, Daniel and Alice shared a look of grim resolve. They knew the road ahead would be treacherous, filled with obstacles and absurdities at every turn. But they also knew that they couldn't sit idly by while their world crumbled around them.

It was time to fight back, to shine a light on the truth no matter how ugly it might be. And with each step they took, their determination only grew stronger, a fire burning in their hearts that refused to be extinguished.

Daniel and Alice burst into Kyle's apartment, the door slamming against the wall with a resounding thud. Kyle, hunched over his workbench, nearly jumped out of his skin at the sudden intrusion. He spun around, a half-assembled gadget clutched in his grease-stained hands.

"What the hell, guys?" he exclaimed, his eyes wide with a mix of surprise and annoyance. "Ever heard of knocking?"

Daniel strode forward, his face a mask of determination. "No time for that, Kyle. We've got big news."

Alice nodded, her expression equally grave. "Brayden Funkledor, our esteemed President-Dictator? He's a fraud. A reality TV star with the IQ of a turnip."

Kyle's jaw dropped, the gadget slipping from his fingers and clattering to the floor. He stared at his friends, his mind reeling as he tried to process the revelation.

"You're shitting me," he said, his voice a hoarse whisper. "That explains so much. The asinine policies, the constant drama, the utter lack of common sense."

Daniel ran a hand through his hair, his eyes darting around the room as if searching for hidden cameras. "We need to expose him, Kyle. This farce has gone on long enough."

Alice leaned against the workbench, her arms crossed over her chest. "But how? The man's got an army of loyal followers, not to mention the media in his pocket."

The trio fell silent, each lost in their own thoughts. The weight of the task before them seemed insurmountable, a Herculean feat in a world gone mad.

Suddenly, Kyle snapped his fingers, his eyes lighting up with a spark of inspiration. "Professor Zander," he said, a grin spreading across his face. "If anyone can help us navigate this shitstorm, it's him."

Daniel and Alice exchanged a look, their own faces mirroring Kyle's excitement. Professor Zander, the eccentric genius who had mentored them all at one point or another. The man was a legend, a brilliant strategist with a knack for thinking outside the box.

"You're right," Daniel said, his voice thrumming with renewed energy. "Zander's our best shot. He'll know what to do."

The trio huddled together, their heads bent in conspiratorial whispers as they brainstormed their next move. The road ahead was certain to be fraught with danger, but they knew they couldn't back down. Not when the fate of their world hung in the balance.

As they made their plans, a sense of purpose filled the air, a palpable electricity that crackled with every word. They were no longer just three friends, but a force to be reckoned with, united in their quest for truth and justice.

And as they set out into the chaotic streets once more, their hearts pounding with a heady mix of fear and determination, they knew that they were ready for whatever lay ahead. Come hell or high water, they would expose Brayden Funkledor for the fraud he was, and restore some semblance of sanity to their dystopian world.

Daniel, Alice, and Kyle hit the streets, their eyes peeled for the first clue that would lead them to Professor Zander. The cryptic message, scrawled on a crumpled piece of paper, had been slipped under Kyle's door just hours before.

"Okay, it says here we need to find the 'Bureaucratic Behemoth,'" Alice said, squinting at the paper. "What the hell does that mean?"

Kyle snapped his fingers. "The Department of Redundancy Department! It's gotta be that government building downtown, the one with the endless lines and the soul-crushing paperwork."

Daniel groaned. "I'd rather face a firing squad than deal with those bureaucratic nightmares again."

But they had no choice. They navigated the labyrinthine streets, dodging street vendors hawking bizarre wares and sidestepping the occasional puddle of questionable origin. The air was thick with the stench of desperation and the cacophony of a city on the brink.

As they approached the towering edifice of the Department of Redundancy Department, they were greeted by a sea of people, all waiting in line with glazed expressions and twitching limbs.

"Holy mother of red tape," Alice muttered, taking in the scene.

They steeled themselves and plunged into the fray, fighting their way through the crowds with a mixture of elbows and apologies. Hours ticked by as they were shuffled from one line to another, each more absurd than the last.

"I'm sorry, but you'll need to fill out Form 27B-6 before we can process your request for Form 92C-1," droned a dead-eyed clerk, his monotone voice barely audible over the din.

Daniel felt his sanity slipping away with each passing minute, but he clung to the thought of Professor Zander and the truth they needed to uncover.

Finally, after what felt like an eternity, they emerged from the bureaucratic hellscape, clutching a small, nondescript envelope.

"If I never see another form again, it'll be too soon," Kyle muttered, wiping the sweat from his brow.

They tore open the envelope, revealing another cryptic clue that led them on a dizzying journey through the city's underbelly. They navigated through dimly lit alleys and abandoned warehouses, encountering a cast of comically exaggerated characters along the way.

There was the old woman who spoke only in riddles, her eyes gleaming with mischief as she sent them on a wild goose chase for a rusted key. And the street performer who insisted on accompanying them with his off-key accordion playing, his antics drawing the attention of every passerby.

But through it all, Daniel, Alice, and Kyle pressed on, their determination never wavering. And finally, as the sun began to set over the city's jagged skyline, they found themselves standing before an inconspicuous door in a rundown building.

Daniel raised his hand, his heart pounding in his chest as he knocked three times, the sound echoing through the empty hallway.

For a moment, there was only silence. And then, the door swung open, revealing the disheveled yet unmistakable figure of Professor Zander.

"Well, well, well," he said, a twinkle in his eye, "look what the dystopian cat dragged in."

The trio stepped into Professor Zander's cluttered office, their eyes widening at the sight of the chaotic mess before them. Papers were strewn across every surface, and half-finished gadgets and contraptions littered the floor.

"Make yourselves at home," Professor Zander said with a grin, gesturing to a worn-out couch that looked like it had seen better days. "Just don't touch anything that looks like it might explode."

Alice raised an eyebrow. "Is that a real possibility?"

"In this world, my dear, anything is possible," Professor Zander replied, his eyes twinkling with mischief.

As they settled in, the professor leaned back in his chair, propping his feet up on a stack of books. "So, you've discovered the truth about our illustrious leader, have you?"

Daniel nodded, his jaw clenched. "We have to do something. We can't let that buffoon continue to run this country into the ground."

Professor Zander stroked his beard, a thoughtful expression on his face. "Ah, but you see, it's not as simple as just exposing him. Brayden's supporters are a loyal bunch, and they'll dismiss anything that doesn't fit their narrative as fake news."

Kyle snorted. "So, what do we do? Just sit back and watch as he turns this place into a reality TV hellscape?"

"Of course not," Professor Zander said, a glint of excitement in his eyes. "We fight fire with fire. We give them a taste of their own medicine."

He leaned forward, his voice lowering to a conspiratorial whisper. "Here's what we're going to do. We're going to create our own fake news broadcast, one that exposes Brayden for the incompetent fool he really is."

Alice frowned. "But won't that just make things worse? Won't people see through it?"

Professor Zander chuckled. "Oh, they'll see through it alright. But that's the beauty of it. We'll make it so ridiculous, so over-the-top, that even Brayden's most ardent supporters will have to question their loyalty."

He grabbed a sheet of paper and began scribbling furiously. "First, we'll need evidence. Documents, recordings, anything that proves Brayden's incompetence. Then, we'll infiltrate the media, plant our story, and watch as it spreads like wildfire."

Daniel's heart raced with excitement. "And then what?"

Professor Zander grinned. "And then, my dear boy, we sit back and watch as the absurdity of it all comes crashing down around them."

The group huddled around Professor Zander's desk, their eyes fixed on the scribbled plan before them. Daniel's mind raced with possibilities, the weight of their mission settling heavily on his shoulders.

"This is insane," Alice muttered, shaking her head. "But damn it, it just might work."

Kyle's eyes sparkled with mischief. "I can already picture Brayden's face when he sees our broadcast. The idiot won't know what hit him."

Professor Zander leaned back in his chair, a satisfied smirk playing on his lips. "Exactly. We'll hit him where it hurts the most—his ego. And once the public sees him for the bumbling fool he is, they'll turn on him faster than you can say 'ratings plummet.'"

Daniel felt a surge of determination coursing through his veins. This was their chance, their opportunity to make a difference in this twisted world. He glanced at his friends, seeing the same resolve etched on their faces.

"Let's do this," he said, his voice steady and unwavering. "Let's take down that reality TV star wannabe and show the world what a real leader looks like."

Alice and Kyle nodded in agreement, their eyes blazing with a newfound sense of purpose. They gathered their belongings, ready to embark on their mission.

As they made their way to the door, Professor Zander called out, "Remember, kids, the key to success is to embrace the absurdity. Use it to your advantage, and never let them see you sweat."

With those parting words ringing in their ears, Daniel, Alice, and Kyle stepped out of the professor's office, their hearts pounding with anticipation. The chaotic streets of the city awaited them, but they were ready to face whatever challenges lay ahead.

Daniel took a deep breath, feeling the weight of the fake news article in his pocket. It was their weapon, their key to exposing Brayden's incompetence to the world.

"Let's give 'em hell," he said, a grin spreading across his face.

And with that, the trio set off into the dystopian landscape, their spirits high and their determination unbreakable. They were ready to take on the absurdity, one ridiculous headline at a time.

The trio stepped out onto the cracked sidewalk, the sun beating down on their faces like a spotlight of ridiculousness. The city was alive with the sounds of honking cars and the chatter of people going about their mundane lives, blissfully unaware of the impending shitstorm that was about to hit them.

"So, where to first?" Kyle asked, his eyes darting around the street, taking in the absurdity that surrounded them.

"We need to find a way to infiltrate the media," Daniel said, his brow furrowed in concentration. "We need to plant our fake news story and make sure it spreads like wildfire."

Alice pulled out her phone, her fingers flying across the screen. "I think I might know someone who can help us with that," she said, a mischievous glint in her eye. "An old friend from my conspiracy theory days. He's got connections in all the right places."

Daniel raised an eyebrow, impressed by Alice's resourcefulness. "Lead the way, then," he said, gesturing for her to take the lead.

As they navigated the streets, dodging the occasional flying burrito wrapper or discarded campaign poster, Daniel couldn't help but feel a sense of exhilaration. They were on a mission, a quest to expose the truth and bring down the absurdity that had taken over their world.

"You know, I never thought I'd be the one to save the world from a reality TV star turned dictator," Kyle mused, his voice laced with amusement. "But here we are, ready to kick some ass and take some names."

Alice snorted, her eyes never leaving her phone. "Better late than never, I suppose," she said, her tone dripping with sarcasm.

As they turned a corner, Daniel caught sight of a group of Brayden's supporters, their faces painted with garish colors and their voices raised in a chant of mindless devotion. He felt a surge of anger, a burning desire to wipe the smug grins off their faces and show them the truth.

"Stay focused," he muttered, more to himself than to the others. "We've got a job to do."

And with that, the trio pressed on, their resolve unshakable as they faced the challenges and absurdities that lay ahead. They were ready to take on the world, one fake news story at a time.

Daniel leaned over the cluttered table in their makeshift headquarters, his brow furrowed as he flipped through the latest stack of Brayden's executive orders. Around him, the faces of his rebel comrades mirrored his own bewilderment and disbelief.

"This can't be for real," muttered Kyle, shaking his head. "The guy's off his rocker."

Alice snatched one of the papers from the pile, her eyes widening as they scanned the text. "Oh, you're gonna love this one. 'Executive Order 451: To promote individuality and self-expression, all citizens are hereby required to wear mismatched socks on Wednesdays. Failure to comply will result in mandatory attendance at a Chuddie rally.'" She looked up, her expression deadpan. "Well, shit. Guess I better start mixing up my sock drawer."

The room erupted into laughter, the absurdity of the situation temporarily overshadowing the gravity of their circumstances. Daniel chuckled, running a hand through his disheveled hair. *How the hell did we end up here?* he wondered, not for the first time. *Living under the rule of a madman, fighting for our right to wear matching socks.*

"I say we start a sock rebellion," Kyle declared, a mischievous glint in his eye. "Wear matching socks every damn day, just to stick it to the man."

"Yeah, that'll show 'em," Alice snorted, rolling her eyes. "Come on, Kyle. We need to focus on the big picture here. Brayden's turning this whole city into a circus, and we're the only ones who seem to give a damn."

Daniel nodded, his amusement fading as the weight of their responsibility settled back onto his shoulders. "Alice is right. We can't get distracted by these ridiculous orders. We need to find a way to expose Brayden for the fraud he is, before it's too late."

He looked around at his fellow rebels, a ragtag group of misfits and outcasts who had somehow become his family. They were all counting on him to lead the way, to find a path through the madness that had engulfed their world.

No pressure, right? Daniel thought wryly. *Just gotta overthrow a tyrannical dictator and restore sanity to a city gone mad. Piece of cake.*

But as he glanced back down at the pile of executive orders, each one more absurd than the last, Daniel felt a flicker of doubt. How were they supposed to fight against something so utterly nonsensical? How could they hope to prevail against an enemy who didn't play by any rules of logic or reason?

One step at a time, he reminded himself, taking a deep breath. *Just keep putting one foot in front of the other, and hope like hell we don't all end up in mismatched socks.*

Amid the laughter and banter, Tim's face paled as he stared at his phone, his finger hovering over the screen. "Uh, guys?" he stammered, drawing the group's attention. "I think I might have accidentally RSVP'd to a Chuddie rally."

The room fell silent for a beat before erupting into a chorus of groans and snickers.

"How the hell do you accidentally RSVP to a Chuddie rally?" Kyle asked, shaking his head in disbelief.

"I was trying to unsubscribe from their mailing list!" Tim protested, his cheeks flushing with embarrassment. "But their website is a mess, and I must have clicked the wrong button."

Alice smirked, her eyes glinting with mischief. "Well, looks like Tim's going to be spending his Saturday with the Chud-heads. Don't forget to wear your best tin foil hat!"

The group erupted into laughter once more, their earlier solemnity forgotten as they teased Tim mercilessly. But Daniel's mind was already racing, a plan forming in his head.

This could be the opportunity we've been waiting for, he mused, his brow furrowing in concentration. *A chance to gather intel on Brayden's supporters, to see what makes them tick.*

He cleared his throat, drawing the group's attention. "Actually, I think Tim should go to the rally," he said, ignoring their incredulous stares. "But not as himself. As an undercover agent."

The group exchanged glances, their expressions ranging from skeptical to intrigued.

"You want me to spy on the Chuddies?" Tim asked, his voice a mix of trepidation and excitement.

Daniel nodded, a grin spreading across his face. "Exactly. We'll arm you with a hidden microphone and a list of questions designed to expose just how absurd this whole thing is. You'll be our eyes and ears on the inside."

The others began to nod, catching on to Daniel's plan.

"We can practice some scenarios," Alice suggested, her eyes sparkling with enthusiasm. "I'll play the role of an overzealous Chuddie, and you can try to get me to say something ridiculous."

She adopted a vacant expression, her voice taking on a monotonous drone. "All hail the great and powerful Brayden, savior of socks and destroyer of rational thought!"

The group burst into laughter once more, the tension in the room dissipating as they began to plan Tim's covert mission.

This is what we're fighting for, Daniel thought, watching his friends banter and scheme. *The right to laugh, to question, to think for ourselves. And we're not going to let some power-hungry madman take that away from us.*

He leaned forward, his eyes glinting with determination. "Alright, let's get to work. Operation Sock Puppet is a go."

The rally was in full swing by the time Tim arrived, his hastily assembled disguise of a fake mustache and oversized sunglasses doing little to calm his nerves. He tugged at the collar of his ill-fitting Brayden t-shirt, wondering how he'd let Daniel talk him into this insanity.

Blend in, he reminded himself, taking a deep breath and plunging into the chaos.

The scene before him was like something out of a fever dream. Hundreds of Chuddies milled about, their faces contorted in expressions of rabid devotion. Off-key chants filled the air, punctuated by the rustling of poorly spelled signs proclaiming Brayden's greatness.

"Socks before talks!" one particularly enthusiastic Chuddie bellowed, thrusting a mismatched pair of socks into the air like a holy relic.

Dear God, what have I gotten myself into? Tim thought, fighting the urge to turn tail and run.

He took a tentative step forward, only to collide with a wiry man in a Brayden hat. The man's eyes widened, his face splitting into a manic grin.

"Brother!" he exclaimed, clapping Tim on the back with enough force to knock the wind out of him. "Have you seen the latest in Brayden merchandise?"

Before Tim could respond, the man was rummaging through a bulging sack, producing a dizzying array of Brayden-themed items. There were Brayden bobbleheads, Brayden keychains, even a Brayden-shaped cake mold.

"I've got it all!" the man crowed, thrusting a Brayden action figure into Tim's hands. "Genuine Chuddie collectibles, straight from the source!"

Tim stared at the action figure, its plastic features frozen in a grotesque approximation of a smile. He could feel the hidden microphone in his pocket, reminding him of his mission.

"Wow," he managed, his voice cracking slightly. "This is... something else."

The man beamed, mistaking Tim's discomfort for admiration. "You ain't seen nothing yet, brother! Wait until you see the limited edition Brayden toilet brush!"

He began to rummage through his sack once more, and Tim seized the opportunity to make his escape. He ducked into the crowd, weaving between the chanting Chuddies with a growing sense of panic.

I'm in over my head, he thought, dodging a particularly enthusiastic sign-waver. *How am I supposed to gather intel when I can barely keep myself from screaming?*

But then he caught sight of a familiar face in the crowd, and his heart nearly stopped. It was Alice, her eyes wide with a mix of amusement and concern. She gave him a subtle nod, and Tim felt a rush of relief.

He wasn't alone in this madness. His friends were counting on him, and he wouldn't let them down. Taking a deep breath, he squared his shoulders and plunged deeper into the rally, determined to see this mission through to the end.

Bring it on, Chuddies, he thought, his lips twisting into a wry smile. *Let's see what other absurdities you've got in store.*

Back at headquarters, Daniel and the others huddled around the speakers, straining to hear Tim's voice amidst the cacophony of the rally. Kyle leaned in, his brow furrowed in concentration, while Alice nervously chewed on her thumbnail.

"Is he... is he talking about a Brayden toilet brush?" Daniel asked incredulously, exchanging a bewildered glance with his companions.

Alice snorted, shaking her head. "I can't believe this is what passes for political discourse these days."

"Hey, don't knock it," Kyle quipped, a mischievous grin spreading across his face. "I hear those toilet brushes are the key to unlocking Brayden's 'visionary' policies."

The group dissolved into laughter, the absurdity of the situation momentarily overshadowing their concern for Tim's safety. Daniel wiped a tear from his eye, struggling to compose himself.

"Okay, okay," he said, waving his hand for quiet. "Let's focus. We need to make sure Tim doesn't get himself into trouble out there."

As if on cue, a new voice crackled through the speakers, causing the group to fall silent. It was a rally organizer, his tone sharp and accusatory.

"You there! I haven't seen you around before. What's your name, brother?"

Tim's voice came through, wavering slightly. "Oh, um... I'm... Lester. Lester Chudson. Huge fan of Brayden's work, really excited to be here today."

The organizer's voice remained skeptical. "Is that so? Well, Lester, perhaps you'd like to share a few words about what Brayden's policies mean to you."

Daniel and the others exchanged worried glances, their hearts pounding. They knew Tim was quick on his feet, but this was a whole new level of pressure.

Come on, Tim, Daniel thought, leaning closer to the speakers. *You've got this. Just channel your inner Chuddie.*

There was a moment of tense silence, broken only by the distant sounds of the rally. Then, Tim's voice rang out, clear and confident.

"Absolutely! Brayden's visionary policies have changed my life, folks. Take his stance on mandatory sock-wearing, for example. It's not just about fashion, it's about freedom. The freedom to express ourselves, to let our individual spirits shine through. And don't even get me started on his groundbreaking work in the field of breakfast cereal regulations..."

As Tim launched into an increasingly nonsensical speech, the group at headquarters struggled to contain their laughter. Kyle buried his face in his hands, his shoulders shaking with mirth, while Alice bit her lip to keep from crying out.

Daniel shook his head in amazement, a grin spreading across his face. Tim was doing it. He was actually pulling it off, spouting absurdities with such conviction that even the suspicious organizer seemed to be buying it.

That's my boy, Daniel thought, a surge of pride welling up in his chest. *Never underestimate the power of a well-placed nonsensical rant.*

As Tim's speech reached a crescendo, the rally erupted into cheers and applause. The group at headquarters exchanged incredulous looks, their laughter giving way to stunned disbelief.

"I can't believe it," Alice muttered, shaking her head. "He actually managed to win them over with that load of bull."

"Never doubt the power of a silver tongue," Daniel replied, a hint of admiration in his voice. "Tim's got a gift for talking his way out of tight spots."

But even as they celebrated Tim's unlikely success, Daniel felt a nagging sense of unease. They were here for a reason, after all, and it wasn't just to poke fun at the Chuddies' expense.

"Alright, folks," he said, his tone growing serious. "Let's not forget why we're here. We need to focus on gathering useful information, anything that might help us take down Brayden and his cronies."

The others sobered up quickly, nodding in agreement. They leaned in closer to the speakers, listening intently as Tim continued to mingle with the crowd.

Just as the rally seemed to be winding down, however, a new commotion arose. The group at headquarters exchanged puzzled glances as they heard the sound of music blaring over the speakers, followed by a chorus of enthusiastic shouts.

"What the hell is going on?" Kyle asked, frowning at the sudden change in atmosphere.

Their question was answered a moment later, as Tim's voice came through the speakers, breathless and incredulous.

"Guys, you're not going to believe this," he said, his words punctuated by bursts of laughter. "But I think I just accidentally started a conga line."

The group stared at each other in disbelief, their jaws dropping open as they processed Tim's words. Sure enough, they could hear the unmistakable sound of a conga beat pulsing in the background, accompanied by the chanting of dozens of voices.

"A conga line?" Alice repeated, her voice rising in pitch. "At a Chuddie rally?"

"Leave it to Tim to turn a political gathering into a dance party," Kyle said, shaking his head in amazement.

As they listened to the bizarre scene unfolding over the speakers, the group couldn't help but dissolve into laughter once again. It was a moment of pure, unadulterated absurdity, a brief respite from the grim realities of their world.

But even as they laughed, Daniel couldn't shake the feeling that their fight was far from over. The Chuddies might be ridiculous, but they were also dangerous, and Brayden's grip on power was only growing stronger by the day.

We'll take our victories where we can get them, he thought, watching as his friends wiped tears of mirth from their eyes. *But we can't lose sight of the bigger picture. The fate of our world depends on it.*

The laughter was still ringing through the air when Tim burst through the door, his face flushed and his eyes wild with excitement. "You guys," he gasped, collapsing into a nearby chair. "You're not gonna believe what just happened."

"Oh, we believe it," Alice said, grinning from ear to ear. "We heard the whole thing over the mic. Nice work starting that conga line, by the way."

Tim groaned, burying his face in his hands. "I didn't mean to! It just sort of...happened."

"Classic Tim," Kyle chuckled, clapping him on the back. "Only you could accidentally start a dance party at a Chuddie rally."

As the group traded jokes and jabs, Daniel leaned forward, his eyes scanning the scattered papers on the table. "Okay, but seriously," he said, "did you manage to gather any useful intel while you were there?"

Tim's face lit up. "Oh man, you should've seen some of the stuff they had for sale. Brayden bobbleheads, Brayden-shaped soap, even Brayden-scented candles. It was like a shrine to the guy."

"Brayden-scented candles?" Alice wrinkled her nose. "I don't even want to know what those smell like."

"Probably like a mixture of bad decisions and cheap hair gel," Kyle quipped, earning a round of snickers from the others.

As the laughter died down, Daniel leaned back in his chair, his expression growing thoughtful. "You know," he said, "as ridiculous as all of this is, we can't forget what we're up against. Brayden and his cronies might be a joke, but they're a dangerous joke. And they're not going to give up power without a fight."

The others nodded, the humor fading from their faces as the weight of their situation settled over them once again.

"So what do we do now?" Alice asked, her voice quiet.

Daniel looked around at his friends, at the determined set of their jaws and the fire in their eyes. "We keep fighting," he said simply. "We keep exposing their lies, keep chipping away at their power base. And most importantly, we keep laughing. Because if we lose our sense of humor, if we let them take away our ability to find joy in the absurdity of it all...then they've already won."

The group was silent for a moment, letting Daniel's words sink in. Then, slowly, smiles began to spread across their faces once more.

"Well then," Tim said, rubbing his hands together with a mischievous grin. "Who's up for a little more undercover work? I hear there's a Chuddie bake sale next week, and I've been practicing my apple pie recipe."

The others groaned, but there was laughter in their voices as they began to plan their next move. The road ahead might be long and the odds stacked against them, but they had each other. And in a world gone mad, that was enough to keep them going, one ridiculous scheme at a time.

Daniel, Alice, Kyle, Liz, and Tim emerged from their beat-up van into a sea of chaos. The rally for Brayden Funkledor was in full swing, his fervent supporters - the Chuddies - packed together like sardines, waving nonsensical signs and chanting slogans that made about as much sense as a screen door on a submarine. The air was thick with the stench of deep fried everything, and Daniel's stomach churned at the thought of choking down another mystery meat on a stick.

Liz shouldered her way through the sweaty crowd, trusty megaphone in hand. She had that look in her eye, the one that said she was about to verbally eviscerate someone. Daniel almost felt sorry for whatever conspiracy theory-spewing Chuddie was about to be on the receiving end. Almost.

"Alright, shitheads, listen up!" Liz's voice boomed out over the din as she climbed onto a makeshift stage cobbled together from rotting pallets and rusted oil drums. "I know y'all are dumber than a sack of hammers, but even you gotta see that this latest steaming pile of bull Brayden's shoveling is grade-A nonsense!"

The Chuddies nearest the stage started booing and jeering, their faces twisted in confusion and anger, as if their two collective brain cells were duking it out for dominance.

This oughta be good, Daniel thought with a smirk, crossing his arms and leaning against a teetering stack of Brayden's latest best-selling manifesto, "Unhinged: A Stable Genius Tells All".

Liz launched into a rapid-fire debunking, laying out facts and logic with the precision of a surgeon and the subtlety of a sledgehammer.

Her voice dripped with sarcasm as she tore apart the latest conspiracy theory that had the Chuddies frothing at the mouth.

"...and so, in conclusion," Liz finished with a flourish, "if you believe any of this steaming crap, congratulations! You're officially too stupid to function in society. Give yourself a round of applause, dipshits!"

The crowd erupted into a cacophony of angry shouts, confused mumbling, and a smattering of hesitant claps from the handful of Chuddies who seemed to be realizing just how ridiculous they sounded.

Daniel glanced around at his friends, their feral grins mirroring his own. In the midst of this idiocracy, they were the only ones keeping any shreds of sanity together. And if that meant verbally bitch-slapping some sense into these walking, talking dumpster fires, then so be it. It was going to be a long, wild ride, but at least they had each other. And a metric shit-ton of snark.

As the confusion rippled through the crowd like a noxious wave, Daniel and Kyle exchanged a knowing look. It was time to strike while the iron was hot, or in this case, while the Chuddies were too busy scratching their heads to put up much of a fight.

"I got the left flank," Kyle said, cracking his knuckles. "You take the right."

"Let's do this," Daniel nodded, a wicked grin spreading across his face.

They waded into the sea of unwashed bodies, the stench of body odor and stale conspiracy theories assaulting their nostrils. Kyle sidled up to a particularly confused-looking Chuddie, his eyes glazed over like a donut left out in the rain.

"Hey, buddy," Kyle said, slinging an arm around the man's shoulders. "You look like you're having a rough time processing all this. Let me break it down for you."

He launched into a rapid-fire explanation, poking holes in the conspiracy theory with the finesse of a drunken acupuncturist. The Chuddie's eyes widened, his mouth hanging open like a broken puppet.

Meanwhile, Daniel had cornered a small group of Chuddies, their expressions ranging from bewildered to downright constipated. He put on his best shit-eating grin, ready to unleash a verbal barrage.

"So, let me get this straight," he began, his voice dripping with sarcasm. "You guys actually believe that Brayden is some sort of secret genius, and all of his batshit insane policies are just part of some grand plan?"

The Chuddies shifted uncomfortably, their eyes darting around like trapped rats. Daniel could practically see the rusty gears turning in their heads, trying to formulate a response.

"Well, I hate to break it to you," he continued, "but the only 'grand plan' Brayden has is to see how far he can shove his head up his own ass before he suffocates."

A few of the Chuddies let out nervous chuckles, while others looked like they were about to cry. Daniel pressed on, his words cutting through their delusions like a rusty chainsaw.

As the minutes ticked by, the crowd's energy began to shift. Pockets of Chuddies were arguing amongst themselves, their voices rising in pitch as they tried to defend their crumbling beliefs. Others simply stood there, mouths agape, as if their brains had short-circuited from the overload of logic and reason.

Daniel and Kyle regrouped, surveying the chaos with a sense of grim satisfaction. It wasn't pretty, but it was a start. They knew they had a long way to go before they could break the Chuddies' stranglehold on reality, but for now, they would take their victories where they could get them.

Even if those victories smelled like a dumpster fire and tasted like stale beer.

Meanwhile, Alice and Tim had set up a small booth nearby, offering free snacks and pamphlets filled with satirical cartoons that lampooned Brayden's policies. The booth quickly became a hotspot for curious Chuddies looking for a break from the chaos.

"Step right up, folks!" Alice called out, her voice dripping with mock enthusiasm. "Get your free 'Brayden's Brain Bites' and learn the truth about our glorious leader!"

The Chuddies approached the booth warily, eyeing the snacks as if they might be laced with cyanide. Tim grinned, holding out a tray of suspiciously lumpy cookies.

"Don't worry, they're not poisoned," he said. "At least, not with anything lethal. The only thing toxic here is Brayden's bullshit."

A few Chuddies snorted, reaching for the cookies with a mix of hunger and morbid curiosity. As they munched on the stale treats, Alice handed out pamphlets, each one featuring a crudely drawn cartoon of Brayden in various compromising positions.

"Read 'em and weep, folks," she said. "Or laugh, if you prefer. Either way, you might learn something."

The Chuddies flipped through the pamphlets, their eyes widening as they took in the scathing satire. Some chuckled nervously, while others looked like they might vomit. But all of them kept reading, unable to look away from the train wreck of truth.

As the booth's popularity grew, the tension in the crowd began to escalate. A group of die-hard Chuddies, led by a particularly loud and obnoxious supporter, stormed towards the stage where Liz was still speaking.

"Shut your mouth, you lying bitch!" the leader screamed, his face red with rage. "Brayden is our savior, and you're just jealous of his greatness!"

The other Chuddies echoed his sentiments, their voices rising in a cacophony of misplaced anger and confusion. They surrounded the stage, jostling each other as they tried to get closer to Liz.

Liz stood her ground, her eyes narrowing as she surveyed the mob. She knew she was in for a fight, but she was ready. She had faced worse than these deluded fools, and she wasn't about to back down now.

"You want the truth?" she shouted, her voice cutting through the noise like a blade. "You can't handle the truth! But I'm going to give it to you anyway, whether you like it or not."

The Chuddies roared, their faces contorted with rage. But Liz just smiled, her eyes glinting with a fierce determination. She had them right where she wanted them, and she was going to make them listen, even if it killed her.

Which, given the looks on some of their faces, it just might.

Liz took a deep breath, then launched into a blistering tirade of witty comebacks and absurd statistics. "Did you know that 87% of conspiracy theories are started by people who still believe in the tooth fairy?" she quipped, her voice dripping with sarcasm. "And that the average Chuddie has an IQ lower than a turnip?"

The Chuddies stared at her, their mouths agape. Some of them looked confused, while others seemed to be struggling to process her words. But a few of the more open-minded ones couldn't help but chuckle at her audacity.

Liz pressed on, her confidence growing with each passing moment. "And let's not forget the time Brayden claimed that the moon was made of cheese," she said, rolling her eyes. "I mean, come on. Even a five-year-old knows that's not true."

The leader of the Chuddies sputtered with rage, his face turning an even deeper shade of red. "Shut up!" he screamed, spittle flying from his lips. "You don't know what you're talking about!"

But Liz just laughed, her voice ringing out across the rally. "Oh, I know exactly what I'm talking about," she retorted. "And so do you, deep down. You just don't want to admit it."

As the argument reached a fever pitch, the large screen behind the stage suddenly flickered to life. The image of Brayden Funkledor himself appeared, his face filling the screen. The Chuddies let out a collective gasp, their eyes widening in awe.

"My fellow Chuddies!" Brayden bellowed, his voice booming through the speakers. "Don't listen to this woman! She's trying to turn you against me with her lies and her fancy book-learning!"

Liz watched in disbelief as Brayden launched into a blustering, incoherent speech, his words tumbling out in a jumble of nonsensical slogans and half-baked ideas. He ranted about the importance of "freedomizing the liberty" and "patriotizing the flag," his face growing redder and more flustered with each passing moment.

The Chuddies stared at the screen, their expressions ranging from confused to utterly baffled. Some of them shifted uncomfortably, as if they were starting to question their blind allegiance to their leader.

Liz saw her chance and seized it. "You see?" she shouted, pointing at the screen. "This is the man you've been following! A bumbling fool who can't even string a coherent sentence together!"

The Chuddies murmured amongst themselves, their voices growing louder and more agitated. Liz watched as the cracks in their unity began to widen, a slow smile spreading across her face. She had them right where she wanted them, and she wasn't about to let up now.

As the chaos crescendoed, Daniel leapt onto the stage, his eyes blazing with determination. He snatched the microphone from Liz's hand and faced the seething crowd, his voice cutting through the cacophony like a razor.

"Listen up, you mouth-breathing, knuckle-dragging troglodytes!" he shouted, his words dripping with sarcasm. "I know it's hard to think with all that empty space between your ears, but try to keep up, will ya?"

The Chuddies fell silent, their jaws slack with shock. Daniel paced the stage, his movements sharp and agitated.

"Your dear leader, the great and powerful Brayden, is nothing more than a two-bit con man with a bad hairpiece and an even worse grasp of reality," he sneered, his lips curling into a mocking grin. "He's been feeding you a steady diet of bullshit and you've been lapping it up like it's the nectar of the gods."

Daniel's words hung in the air, the tension palpable. The Chuddies shifted restlessly, their eyes darting between the stage and the screen where Brayden's face still loomed, frozen in a comical expression of outrage.

"But here's the thing," Daniel continued, his voice dropping to a conspiratorial whisper. "You don't have to live like this. You don't have to be mindless drones, blindly following a madman into oblivion. You have the power to think for yourselves, to question the absurdity of this world and demand something better."

He paused, letting his words sink in. The Chuddies stared at him, their faces a mix of confusion and dawning realization.

"So what do you say?" Daniel asked, spreading his arms wide. "Are you ready to break free from the shackles of stupidity and embrace the glorious chaos of independent thought? Or are you content to wallow in ignorance, forever chained to the whims of a delusional despot?"

The crowd erupted into a frenzy of shouts and cheers, some Chuddies pumping their fists in the air while others looked around in bewilderment. Daniel grinned, basking in the mayhem he had unleashed.

Amidst the pandemonium, Alice and Tim moved through the crowd, their arms laden with pamphlets. They weaved between the Chuddies, thrusting the satirical literature into their hands with a fervor that bordered on manic.

"Educate yourselves, you glorious bastards!" Alice shouted, her voice barely audible over the din. "These pamphlets hold the key to your liberation!"

Tim nodded enthusiastically, his face flushed with excitement. "It's time to break free from the chains of ignorance and embrace the sweet, sweet chaos of knowledge!"

The Chuddies grabbed at the pamphlets, their eyes widening as they took in the biting satire and scathing cartoons. Some laughed uproariously, their faces contorted with glee, while others furrowed their brows, struggling to comprehend the subversive message.

"Wait a minute," one Chuddie said, scratching his head. "Are you saying that Brayden's been lying to us this whole time?"

"Of course he has, you dolt!" another Chuddie retorted, smacking him upside the head with a pamphlet. "Haven't you been paying attention?"

The rally descended into a chaotic mess of arguments and debates, Chuddies shouting over each other as they tried to make sense of the new information. Some clung stubbornly to their beliefs, their faces twisted with anger and denial, while others embraced the chaos, their laughter ringing out across the crowd.

Daniel watched from the stage, a satisfied smirk playing across his lips. He knew that this was only the beginning, that there was still a long way to go before the Chuddies truly broke free from Brayden's grip. But for now, he reveled in the small victory, the knowledge that he had planted the seeds of doubt and dissent in the minds of the masses.

As the rally devolved into a raucous cacophony of conflicting ideas and opinions, Daniel couldn't help but feel a sense of pride. They had started something here, something that could potentially change the course of their dystopian world. And even if it all ended in disaster, at least they could say they had tried, that they had fought against the absurdity with everything they had.

Daniel hopped off the stage, weaving through the throng of confused Chuddies, and rejoined his companions. They huddled together, their faces flushed with adrenaline and excitement.

"Did you see that?" Alice grinned, her eyes sparkling with mischief. "They're actually thinking for themselves!"

"I never thought I'd see the day," Kyle chuckled, shaking his head in disbelief.

Liz threw an arm around Daniel's shoulders, giving him a playful squeeze. "Not bad, fearless leader. You really know how to work a crowd."

Daniel shrugged, trying to play it cool, but he couldn't hide the pride that swelled in his chest. "I just told them the truth. It's not my fault if they couldn't handle it."

Tim snorted, his lips twitching with amusement. "Yeah, well, let's just hope they don't come after us with pitchforks and torches later."

The group shared a laugh, the tension of the rally melting away as they basked in their shared triumph. For a moment, they could forget about the bleak reality of their world, the constant threat of Brayden's tyranny, and simply enjoy each other's company.

As the Chuddies began to disperse, some still arguing amongst themselves, others wandering off in a daze, the rally took on a surreal quality. The once-imposing screens now displayed nothing but static, Brayden's face frozen in a comical expression of confusion and rage.

Daniel took a deep breath, savoring the chaos, the feeling of having made a difference, however small. He knew that tomorrow would bring new challenges, new obstacles to overcome, but for now, he allowed himself to hope, to believe that change was possible.

The chapter closed on a scene of beautiful disarray, the Chuddies stumbling away from the rally, their world turned upside down by a few well-placed words and a healthy dose of laughter. And as Daniel and his friends walked off into the sunset, ready to face whatever came next, the reader couldn't help but feel a sense of kinship with these unlikely heroes, these brave souls who dared to stand up against the absurdity of their dystopian reality.

Daniel slumped on the rickety park bench, its splintered wood digging into his ass as he watched the world unravel before his bloodshot eyes. Across the patchy grass, Alice and Kyle huddled over a crumpled government pamphlet, their faces scrunched in comic befuddlement as they tried to decipher its bureaucratic word salad.

Daniel snorted. Good luck with that, he thought. Trying to make sense of Brayden's regime was like attempting to teach a cat to juggle chainsaws - an exercise in futility and lost fingers.

His gaze drifted to the propaganda posters plastered on the graffitied walls, their bright colors and cheery slogans a mocking contrast to the gray despair that choked the city. "A Smile A Day Keeps The Dissent Away!" one proclaimed, featuring a grinning, soulless face.

Daniel's lip curled. What a load of horseshit. He'd seen firsthand how quickly those mandatory smiles evaporated under the regime's iron fist. The bruises hidden beneath ill-fitting uniforms, the haunted eyes of those who dared to question or resist.

And for what? He wondered bitterly. What difference could their little band of misfits really make against the might of Brayden's brainwashed goon squad? They were just a bunch of jaded twentysomethings with more snark than sense, tilting at dystopian windmills.

"Hey, check this out!" Kyle's voice cut through Daniel's glum reverie. He waved the pamphlet like a manic town crier. "According to this, excessive frowning is now punishable by a mandatory week-long laughter therapy retreat!"

Alice snatched the paper, her eyes bugging out. "Holy hell, it gets better. Failure to respond to the daily 'Joy Inspections' with sufficient enthusiasm will result in immediate relocation to a government-approved 'Happiness Camp' for attitude realignment!"

They dissolved into snickers, their laughter tinged with an edge of hysteria. Daniel just shook his head, a wry smile tugging at his mouth despite himself. In a world gone mad, gallows humor was the only sane response left.

But beneath the laughter, the doubts gnawed at him like rats in the walls of his mind. How long could they keep this up, this absurd game of pretend rebellion? Sooner or later, Brayden's goons would kick down their doors and drag them off to some godforsaken humor gulag, never to be seen again.

Daniel sighed, his shoulders sagging under the weight of futility. Maybe it was time to stop fighting the insanity and just embrace the brain-melting absurdity of it all. Don a clown nose, spout some approved witticisms, and shuffle along like the rest of the grinning zombies.

After all, if you can't beat 'em, join 'em. Resistance was starting to feel as pointless as a whoopee cushion in a hurricane. In the end, they were all just rats trapped in the same cosmic joke of a maze, scurrying towards the illusory promise of cheese.

With a grunt, Daniel heaved himself off the bench and ambled towards his friends, resigned to another day of pissing into the wind of tyranny. The pamphlet crinkled in his fist, a perverse reminder of the uphill battle they faced.

But hell, at least they had each other - a ragtag band of smartasses united in their refusal to go quietly into the dystopian night. If they were going down, they'd do it laughing, with a defiant middle finger raised to the powers that be.

It wasn't much, but in this screwed-up world, gallows humor and a touch of insanity might just be their only hope of staying sane.

Alice glanced up from the pamphlet, her brow furrowed with concern as she caught sight of Daniel's distant expression. She nudged Kyle, jerking her head towards their brooding friend.

"Hey, check out Mr. Sunshine over there," she quipped, her voice dripping with sarcasm. "I think he's having a moment."

Kyle followed her gaze, a lopsided grin spreading across his face. "Probably trying to decide which color of jumpsuit brings out his eyes. I hear the new 'Obedient Citizen Gray' is all the rage this season."

They snickered, the sound a brief respite from the oppressive atmosphere. Alice crumpled the pamphlet into a ball and tossed it over her shoulder with a flourish.

"C'mon, let's go cheer him up before he starts writing angsty poetry or something," she said, dragging Kyle towards the bench.

As they approached, Alice draped an arm around Daniel's shoulders, jostling him out of his reverie. "So, did you hear about the latest executive order? Apparently, we're all required to wear propeller hats on Tuesdays to boost morale."

Kyle chimed in, his eyes twinkling with mischief. "Yeah, and failure to comply results in mandatory attendance at a 24-hour seminar on the importance of conformity. I hear they serve stale crackers and lukewarm water."

Their laughter echoed through the park, a fleeting moment of normalcy in a world gone mad. But Daniel remained silent, his gaze fixed on the ground, lost in the labyrinth of his own thoughts.

Suddenly, a figure emerged from the chaos, his appearance so bizarre that it momentarily jolted Daniel back to reality. Professor Zander strode towards them, his mismatched socks peeking out from beneath his trousers, a hat that looked suspiciously like a repurposed circus tent perched jauntily on his head.

He approached the trio with a knowing grin, his eyes twinkling with a mix of mischief and understanding as he sensed the storm clouds gathering in Daniel's mind. Zander clapped a hand on the young man's shoulder, his grip firm and reassuring.

"Ah, the intrepid rebels," he declared, his voice carrying a hint of grandeur. "Plotting your next move against the forces of absurdity, I presume?"

Daniel looked up, meeting Zander's gaze with a wry smile. "More like contemplating the futility of it all, Professor. Sometimes it feels like we're just tilting at windmills."

Zander chuckled, a deep, rich sound that seemed to emanate from his very core. He leaned in conspiratorially, his eyes darting left and right as if checking for eavesdroppers.

"Ah, but remember, my dear boy," he whispered, his voice laced with a peculiar blend of wisdom and whimsy, "even the most formidable windmill can be toppled with the right approach. And I have a feeling that you three might just be the ones to do it."

Daniel couldn't help but roll his eyes at the professor's bizarre analogy. "Toppling windmills? Is that your idea of a pep talk, Zander?"

"Think about it," Zander insisted, his hands gesticulating wildly as if conducting an invisible orchestra. "Windmills seem imposing, right? All tall and spinny and intimidating. But what are they, really? Just a bunch of gears and blades, held together by a few bolts and a prayer."

Despite his skepticism, Daniel found himself intrigued by the professor's unconventional perspective. He leaned forward, his brow furrowed in thought. "So, what you're saying is...?"

"What I'm saying, dear boy, is that even the most daunting challenges can be overcome if you approach them with the right mindset. Take Brayden's regime, for example. Sure, it seems like an unassailable fortress of bureaucratic bullshit, but even the mightiest fortress has its cracks."

Zander's eyes sparkled with a mischievous glint as he continued, "And that's where you three come in. You're the ones who can find those cracks, the ones who can exploit the weaknesses in the system. It won't be easy, mind you. You'll have to be clever, resourceful, and maybe a little bit insane. But if anyone can do it, it's you lot."

Daniel couldn't suppress a smirk at the professor's words. As much as he wanted to dismiss them as the ramblings of an eccentric old man, there was a certain truth to them that resonated deep within him.

"Alright, Professor," he conceded, his tone still tinged with skepticism. "Let's say we are the ones to take on this windmill of a regime. How exactly do we go about doing that?"

Zander grinned, a glint of mischief dancing in his eyes. "Ah, that's the beauty of it, my boy. There's no one right answer. You'll have to get creative, think outside the box. Use the very absurdity of the system against itself."

He leaned in closer, his voice dropping to a conspiratorial whisper. "Imagine, for a moment, a world where the most ridiculous ideas are the ones that carry the most weight. A world where the only way to fight nonsense is with even greater nonsense. That, my dear Daniel, is the key to toppling this particular windmill."

Daniel couldn't help but be drawn in by the professor's words, as bizarre as they seemed. His mind raced with possibilities, each more outlandish than the last. Perhaps there was something to this whole embracing-the-absurdity thing after all.

Professor Zander reached into his tattered satchel and pulled out a rubber chicken and a yo-yo. He held them up triumphantly, as if they were the keys to unlocking the secrets of the universe. "Behold, the tools of our revolution!"

Alice and Kyle exchanged amused glances, their eyebrows raised in disbelief. Daniel, despite his earlier skepticism, found himself leaning forward, curiosity piqued.

"Now, observe closely," Zander instructed, his voice taking on a theatrical quality. He began to yo-yo with one hand while simultaneously squeezing the rubber chicken with the other. The chicken let out a series of comical squawks, perfectly timed with the yo-yo's ups and downs.

"Life, my dear friends," Zander declared, "is a delicate balance between the absurd and the profound. Just like this yo-yo and chicken, we must learn to navigate the chaos, to find harmony in the discord."

As the professor continued his bizarre demonstration, Daniel couldn't help but chuckle. The sight of this eccentric man, with his mismatched socks and clownish hat, imparting wisdom through a rubber chicken and a yo-yo, was too much to bear.

And yet, as he watched, a strange realization began to dawn on him. Perhaps there was a method to Zander's madness. In a world where nothing made sense, where the rules were constantly shifting, maybe the only way to survive was to embrace the chaos, to find the humor in the absurdity.

Leave it to Zander to find enlightenment in a damn rubber chicken, Daniel thought, shaking his head in amusement. *But hell, if it works, who am I to argue?*

As the demonstration came to a close, with Zander bowing dramatically and the chicken letting out one final, indignant squawk, Daniel felt a weight lifting from his shoulders. The problems they faced were still there, looming large and seemingly insurmountable, but somehow, they felt a little less daunting.

Maybe that's the secret, he mused, watching as Alice and Kyle applauded the professor's performance. *Maybe the key to surviving in this messed-up world is to stop trying to make sense of it all and just roll with the punches. Embrace the chaos, find the humor in the darkness, and keep on fighting, one ridiculous step at a time.*

Zander plopped down on the bench beside Daniel, the rubber chicken dangling from his hand. "You know," he said, his voice taking on a more somber tone, "I wasn't always this way. I used to be just like you, kid. Serious, focused, determined to make a difference."

Daniel raised an eyebrow. "You? Serious? I find that hard to believe."

Zander chuckled. "Believe it or not, there was a time when I wouldn't be caught dead with a rubber chicken. I was a young idealist, full of grand ideas about changing the world. But then, well, the world changed me."

He paused, his eyes growing distant. "It was during the early days of Brayden's regime. I was part of a resistance group, much like you and your friends. We had plans, strategies, a vision for a better future. But with each passing day, things just got more and more absurd."

Daniel leaned forward, intrigued. He had never heard Zander speak about his past before.

"We tried to fight it at first," Zander continued, "tried to cling to our sense of normalcy. But it was like trying to hold onto a fistful of sand. The more we struggled, the more it slipped through our fingers. And then, one day, I just... let go."

He looked at Daniel, a hint of mischief returning to his eyes. "I realized that the only way to survive in a world gone mad was to embrace the madness. To find the humor in the darkness, the absurdity in the chaos. And you know what? It worked."

Daniel felt a sudden kinship with the eccentric professor. He had always seen Zander as a bit of a mystery, a wild card in their fight against Brayden. But now, he began to understand. Zander wasn't just some crazy old man with a penchant for rubber chickens. He was a survivor, someone who had learned to adapt to the insanity of their world.

"I guess what I'm trying to say," Zander concluded, "is that you're not alone in this, kid. We're all in the same boat, paddling upstream in a river of nonsense. But if we stick together, if we learn to laugh in the face of the absurd, we just might make it through to the other side."

He stood up, stretching his long limbs. "Now, if you'll excuse me, I have a very important meeting with a whoopee cushion and a can of silly string. Remember, Daniel: embrace the chaos. It's the only way to stay sane in an insane world."

As Zander ambled off, Daniel felt a newfound sense of camaraderie with the old professor. He glanced over at Alice and Kyle, who were still engrossed in their attempt to decipher the government pamphlet. Maybe Zander was right. Maybe the key to surviving in this dystopian nightmare was to stop trying to make sense of it all and start finding the humor in the absurdity.

Embrace the chaos, he thought, a small smile tugging at the corners of his mouth. *Why the hell not? It's not like anything else has worked so far.*

With a renewed sense of determination, Daniel stood up and joined his friends, ready to face whatever ridiculous challenges the world had in store for them next. Together, they would fight the good fight, one rubber chicken at a time.

Alice looked up from the pamphlet, her eyes sparkling with mischief. "You know, I think Zander's onto something. If we can't beat 'em, why not join 'em in the madness?"

Kyle snorted. "What, like start our own absurdist resistance movement? The Revolutionary Rubber Chicken Brigade?"

"Why not?" Alice grinned. "We could stage elaborate pranks, leave cryptic messages in whoopee cushions... Brayden would never know what hit him!"

Daniel couldn't help but chuckle at the image of Brayden's stern face covered in silly string. "You know, that's not half bad. We could use some levity in this fight."

Kyle tossed the pamphlet aside, a smile spreading across his face. "Alright, I'm in. But I get to be the one who puts the whoopee cushion on Brayden's throne."

As they laughed, Daniel felt a warmth spreading through his chest. Maybe this was what Zander meant about the power of friendship in the face of adversity. They might be just a ragtag bunch of misfits, but together, they could take on anything - even a totalitarian regime with a penchant for the bizarre.

"Okay, team," Daniel said, his voice filled with a newfound sense of purpose. "Let's do this. Let's show Brayden that he can't crush our spirits, no matter how hard he tries."

Alice pumped her fist in the air. "The Revolutionary Rubber Chicken Brigade, reporting for duty!"

As they set off into the chaotic streets, armed with nothing but their wits and a healthy dose of absurdity, Daniel couldn't help but feel a glimmer of hope. Sure, the world might be a mess, but with his friends by his side, he knew they could face anything.

Bring it on, Brayden, he thought, a smirk playing at his lips. *We're ready for you.*

Professor Zander, having imparted his peculiar wisdom, turned to make his exit with a flourish. He swirled his mismatched coat, the tails flapping in the wind like a demented magician's cape. With a wink and a grin, he declared, "Remember, my young revolutionaries, chaos is merely order's eccentric cousin. Embrace the madness, and you'll find your path to victory!"

He took a step forward, his head held high, ready to vanish into the dystopian landscape like a mythical figure of legend. However, fate had other plans. Zander's foot caught on a crack in the pavement, and he stumbled, his arms pinwheeling in a desperate attempt to maintain balance.

So much for a grand exit, Daniel thought, stifling a laugh as he watched his mentor flail about like a drunken flamingo.

Zander, ever the performer, managed to turn his tumble into an impromptu somersault, landing in a crouched position with his arms spread wide. "Ta-da!" he exclaimed, as if he had just executed a flawless acrobatic maneuver.

Alice and Kyle burst into laughter, their voices ringing out amidst the cacophony of the city. Daniel shook his head, a grin spreading across his face. *Leave it to Zander to find humor in the most unexpected places.*

As Zander dusted himself off, his hat askew and his dignity only slightly bruised, Daniel realized that this moment encapsulated the very essence of their struggle. In a world gone mad, where absurdity reigned supreme, sometimes the only way to survive was to embrace the chaos and find the laughter hidden within.

We might be living in a dystopian nightmare, Daniel mused, *but as long as we have each other, and a healthy dose of humor, we can face anything.*

With renewed determination, Daniel rose from the bench, ready to tackle whatever bizarre challenges lay ahead. He knew that the road to overthrow Brayden's regime would be long and treacherous, but with his friends by his side and a spring in his step, he felt invincible.

Bring it on, world, he thought, his eyes sparkling with mischief. *The Revolutionary Rubber Chicken Brigade is ready to ruffle some feathers.*

The flickering fluorescent bulb cast an eerie glow over the cramped room, illuminating the determined faces of Daniel and his ragtag crew. Empty pizza boxes littered the floor, their greasy scent mingling with the musty air. Daniel leaned forward, his elbows resting on his knees. "Alright, let's hear some ideas. How do we take down that pompous windbag Brayden Funkledor?"

Alice twirled a strand of blue hair around her finger. "We could hack into his personal files, dig up some dirty secrets."

"Nah, too risky," Kyle said, lounging back in his chair. "I say we stage a protest, make a big scene outside his office. Maybe throw some rotten eggs for good measure."

Liz snorted. "Yeah, because that worked so well last time. I still have bruises from those riot batons."

Tim, ever the pragmatist, chimed in. "What about a petition? We could gather signatures, show the people are united against him."

Daniel sighed, rubbing his temples. The ideas swirled in his mind, each one more far-fetched than the last. They needed something bold, something that would hit Brayden where it hurt. But what?

Suddenly, the door burst open, and in strode Professor Zander, his wild gray hair sticking out in all directions. He let out a cackle, his eyes sparkling with mischief. "I've got it!" he exclaimed, clapping his hands together. "A fake news broadcast! We'll expose Brayden's incompetence to the world!"

The room fell silent, everyone staring at Zander like he'd grown a second head. Daniel felt a flicker of doubt. A fake news broadcast? It sounded absurd, even by their standards. But as he mulled it over, a grin spread across his face. Maybe, just maybe, it was crazy enough to work.

"I like it," Daniel said, standing up. "It's bold, it's unexpected, and it'll hit Brayden right where it hurts - his ego."

Alice raised an eyebrow. "And how exactly are we supposed to pull off a fake news broadcast?"

Zander waved his hand dismissively. "Details, details! We'll figure it out as we go along. The important thing is, we've got a plan."

As the group began to buzz with excitement, throwing out ideas and suggestions, Daniel felt a surge of energy coursing through his veins. This was it, their chance to strike back against the tyranny of Brayden Funkledor. And with Professor Zander's mad genius on their side, anything was possible.

Daniel clapped his hands, calling the room to attention. "Alright, folks, let's get to work. We've got a broadcast to plan and a dictator to take down. Time to show Brayden what happens when you mess with the resistance."

As they dove into the planning, Daniel couldn't help but feel a flicker of hope amidst the chaos. Maybe, just maybe, they could pull this off. And even if they failed, at least they'd go down swinging, with laughter on their lips and defiance in their hearts.

Alice's fingers flew across the keyboard, her brow furrowed in concentration as she worked on creating the fake news graphics. "How's this?" she asked, spinning the laptop around to reveal a convincing news banner emblazoned with the words "BREAKING NEWS: BRAYDEN FUNKLEDOR'S SECRET SCANDAL EXPOSED."

Kyle grinned, rubbing his hands together. "Perfect. I can already see myself delivering this report with Oscar-worthy gravitas."

"You? Oscar-worthy?" Liz scoffed, rolling her eyes. "More like Razzie-worthy."

Tim chuckled, reaching for a slice of pizza, but accidentally knocked over his soda can in the process. The sugary liquid splashed across the plans scattered on the table, prompting a chorus of groans and laughter.

"Way to go, Tim," Liz sighed, dabbing at the papers with a napkin. "Now our plans are sticky and smell like root beer."

"Hey, it adds character," Tim shrugged, unapologetic. "Besides, a little chaos never hurt anyone."

As the group worked, the room hummed with an odd mix of determination and hilarity. Kyle rehearsed his lines, pacing back and forth with exaggerated seriousness, while Alice tinkered with the graphics, adding increasingly absurd elements to the fake news story.

"What if we say Brayden has a secret collection of porcelain dolls that he talks to for advice?" Alice suggested, her eyes sparkling with mischief.

Daniel couldn't help but laugh. "I like it. It's just the right amount of ridiculous."

The hours ticked by, the stale pizza growing colder and the empty soda cans piling up. But despite the fatigue and the occasional bouts of frustration, the group remained united in their purpose. They were in this together, bound by a shared desire to take down Brayden and restore some semblance of sanity to their dystopian world.

As Daniel watched his friends work, he felt a swell of affection and gratitude. Sure, they were a ragtag bunch of misfits, but they were his misfits. And together, they just might have a shot at pulling off the impossible.

The scene was set, the players in place. All that remained was to put their plan into action and hope for the best. It was a long shot, but in a world gone mad, sometimes the most absurd ideas were the only ones that made sense.

Daniel took a deep breath, steeling himself for the challenges ahead. "Alright, team," he said, his voice ringing with determination. "Let's do this. Let's show Brayden Funkledor what happens when you underestimate the power of a bunch of crazy, pizza-fueled rebels with a dream."

And with that, they plunged headlong into their mad scheme, laughter and hope mingling in the air, a defiant light amidst the darkness of their dystopian reality.

Daniel leaned back in his chair, the weight of leadership heavy on his shoulders. He watched as his friends rehearsed their roles, a spark of pride igniting in his chest. Kyle, ever the dramatic one, delivered his lines with an exaggerated flair that bordered on the ridiculous.

"I've seen things, man," Kyle bellowed, his face contorted into a mask of feigned anguish. "Things that would make your skin crawl and your balls shrivel up like raisins."

Liz snorted, rolling her eyes. "Easy there, Marlon Brando. We're trying to expose a corrupt politician, not audition for a soap opera."

Kyle shot her a grin, undeterred. "Hey, if we're gonna do this, we might as well do it with style."

As the group dissolved into laughter, Daniel's thoughts drifted to Professor Zander and his unconventional wisdom. The eccentric academic had a way of putting things into perspective, even in the most absurd situations. Daniel could almost hear his voice now, a mischievous lilt to his words.

"Remember, my dear boy," Professor Zander would say, "sometimes the most ridiculous ideas are the most effective. It's like trying to catch a fish with a banana - it's so unexpected that it just might work."

Daniel shook his head, a smile tugging at his lips. Leave it to Professor Zander to compare their plan to fishing with fruit. But as he watched his friends work, their determination unwavering even in the face of their own laughter, he couldn't help but feel a glimmer of hope.

Alice, her brow furrowed in concentration, tapped away at her laptop, perfecting the digital effects that would sell their story. The glow of the screen cast an eerie light on her face, but her eyes sparkled with a fierce intelligence.

"How's it coming, Alice?" Daniel asked, leaning over her shoulder.

"Almost there," she replied, her fingers flying across the keys. "Just need to add a few more touches to make it look like Brayden's head is actually up his own ass."

Daniel chuckled, marveling at her skill. "You're a genius, you know that?"

Alice flashed him a grin. "Tell me something I don't know."

As the night wore on, the group continued to rehearse, their laughter punctuated by moments of intense focus. Tim, ever the klutz, managed to knock over a stack of papers, sending them fluttering to the floor like oversized confetti.

"Shit, sorry," he mumbled, scrambling to pick them up.

But even as they ribbed him good-naturedly, the group remained united in their purpose. They were a team, bound by a shared goal and an unshakeable bond of friendship.

And as Daniel watched them work, he felt a surge of confidence. Maybe, just maybe, they could pull this off. Maybe their ridiculous plan, born of desperation and fueled by laughter, could actually make a difference.

It was a long shot, but in a world gone mad, sometimes the most absurd ideas were the only ones that made sense. And with his friends by his side, Daniel was ready to take on whatever the dystopian world threw their way, one ridiculous scheme at a time.

The deadline loomed, and Daniel felt a knot of doubt tighten in his gut. He stared at the chaos before him—the tangle of wires, the haphazard props, the hastily scrawled cue cards—and wondered if they were in over their heads.

Professor Zander, as if sensing his hesitation, sidled up beside him. "You know, Daniel," he said, his voice low and conspiratorial, "penguins have a lot to teach us about perseverance."

Daniel raised an eyebrow. "Penguins?"

"Oh, yes." Zander nodded sagely. "You see, when a penguin wants to catch a fish, it doesn't just give up after one try. It dives in again and again, no matter how cold the water or how elusive the prey."

He fixed Daniel with a piercing stare. "And that's what we're doing here, my boy. We're diving in, again and again, until we catch our fish. Or, in this case, until we expose Brayden Funkledor for the bumbling buffoon he is."

Daniel couldn't help but crack a smile. Leave it to Zander to find inspiration in the most unlikely of places. "Thanks, Professor," he said. "I needed that."

Zander clapped him on the shoulder. "Anytime, my boy. Anytime."

With renewed determination, Daniel turned to face the group. "All right, everyone," he called out, his voice ringing with authority. "Let's run through it one more time. From the top."

They scrambled into position, a ragtag crew of misfits and dreamers. Kyle took his place behind the makeshift anchor desk, straightening his tie with exaggerated gravitas. Alice hovered over her computer, her fingers flying across the keyboard as she made last-minute adjustments to the graphics.

Liz and Tim flanked the green screen, armed with an assortment of props and costumes. They exchanged a glance, their eyes sparkling with mischief and anticipation.

"And... action!" Daniel called out.

The room buzzed with energy as they launched into their final rehearsal. Kyle delivered his lines with a perfect mix of sincerity and absurdity, his voice dripping with mock outrage. Alice's graphics flashed across the screen, each one more ridiculous than the last.

And through it all, Daniel watched with a sense of pride and wonder. This was his team, his friends, his partners in crime. Together, they were unstoppable.

The scene ended with a final flourish, and the group erupted into applause and laughter. They had done it. They were ready.

Daniel took a deep breath, feeling the weight of responsibility settle on his shoulders. It was time to take the fight to Brayden Funkledor, to expose his incompetence and bring a glimmer of hope to their dystopian world.

And with his friends by his side, he knew they could do anything. Even if it meant diving in, again and again, like a penguin chasing its prey.

The broadcast began with a flicker of static, the screen cutting to Kyle, who sat behind a makeshift news desk, his face a mask of grave concern. "Good evening, citizens," he intoned, his voice deep and commanding. "Tonight, we bring you an exclusive report on the shocking incompetence of our so-called leader, Brayden Funkledor."

Behind the camera, Daniel watched, his heart pounding in his chest. This was it. The moment of truth.

As Kyle launched into his script, the screen behind him burst to life, displaying a series of graphs and charts, each one more absurd than the last. "As you can see," Kyle continued, gesturing to a pie chart that showed Brayden's approval rating hovering at a measly 2%, "our fearless leader has been failing us at every turn."

The broadcast cut to a series of doctored footage, showing Brayden stumbling through press conferences, tripping over his own feet, and accidentally setting fire to his own toupee. Daniel couldn't help but snicker at the sight, even as his stomach churned with nerves.

Next to him, Alice, Liz, and Tim watched the broadcast with bated breath, their eyes glued to the screen. They had poured their hearts and souls into this plan, and now, as it unfolded before them, they could only hope that it would be enough.

As the broadcast wore on, Kyle's performance grew more and more outrageous, his voice rising to a fever pitch as he railed against Brayden's incompetence. "And let's not forget," he shouted, slamming his fist on the desk, "the time he tried to solve our energy crisis by harnessing the power of hamster wheels!"

Daniel felt a surge of pride as he watched his friend work the camera, his face a mask of righteous indignation. Kyle was a natural, and with Alice's graphics and Liz and Tim's props, the broadcast looked almost professional. Almost.

But even as they reveled in their small victory, Daniel couldn't shake the feeling of unease that settled in the pit of his stomach. This was just the beginning, he knew. Brayden wouldn't take this lying down, and they would have to be ready for whatever came next.

As the broadcast drew to a close, Kyle delivered his final line with a flourish. "And so, dear citizens, I ask you this: are you ready for a change? Are you ready to take back control of our city, our lives, our future?"

The screen faded to black, and for a moment, the room was silent. Then, slowly, the group began to cheer, their voices rising in a chorus of victory.

Daniel felt a hand on his shoulder and turned to see Professor Zander standing behind him, a proud smile on his face. "Well done, my boy," he said, his eyes twinkling with mischief. "You've struck a blow against the establishment, and you've done it with style."

Daniel grinned, feeling a rush of adrenaline coursing through his veins. They had done it. They had taken their first step towards bringing down Brayden Funkledor, and they had done it together.

But even as they celebrated, Daniel knew that the real battle was just beginning. They would have to be ready for whatever came next, whatever absurdity the dystopian world threw their way.

But for now, in this moment, they could revel in their triumph, in the knowledge that they had made a difference. And that, Daniel thought, was worth all the stale pizza and spilled soda in the world.

The group's phones suddenly erupted in a cacophony of buzzes and pings, their screens lighting up with notifications. Alice's eyes widened as she scrolled through her feed. "Holy shit, guys! The broadcast is going viral!"

Kyle snatched his phone, his jaw dropping. "Look at these numbers! We're trending on every platform!"

Liz leaned over his shoulder, a smirk playing on her lips. "Who would've thought that our little fake news stunt would strike such a chord?"

Tim chuckled, shaking his head in disbelief. "I guess people are just desperate for some truth in this messed-up world."

Daniel stood back, watching as his friends reveled in their newfound fame. The absurdity of the situation wasn't lost on him. Here they were, a group of misfits who had just challenged the status quo with nothing more than a green screen and some clever editing.

But as he looked around at their faces, at the determination and the humor that shone in their eyes, he felt a swell of pride. They had done something that mattered, something that could change the course of their lives and the lives of everyone in the city.

"We did it," he said, his voice barely above a whisper. "We actually fucking did it."

Professor Zander clapped him on the back, his laughter booming through the room. "And you thought my idea was crazy! Never underestimate the power of a well-timed joke, my boy."

Daniel shook his head, a grin spreading across his face. "I should've known better than to doubt you, Professor. You're the master of the absurd."

As the group continued to celebrate, their phones buzzing with each new notification, Daniel couldn't help but marvel at the sheer ridiculousness of it all. They were just a bunch of college kids, armed with nothing but their wits and their determination. And yet, somehow, they had managed to strike a blow against the most powerful man in the city.

It was a reminder, he thought, that even in the darkest of times, there was always hope. And as long as they had each other, as long as they were willing to fight for what they believed in, anything was possible.

Even taking down a tyrannical ruler with a fake news broadcast and a whole lot of humor.

Professor Zander raised his glass, the amber liquid sloshing dangerously close to the rim. "A toast," he declared, his eyes twinkling with mischief, "to the bravest, most ingenious group of troublemakers I've ever had the pleasure of mentoring."

The group gathered around, their own glasses held high. Alice, her face illuminated by the glow of her laptop screen, grinned broadly. "To taking down the man with nothing but our wit and a green screen!"

"And don't forget the power of Kyle's acting skills," Liz chimed in, elbowing the aspiring thespian playfully. "Who knew he could look so convincing as a disgruntled government employee?"

Kyle took a dramatic bow, nearly spilling his drink in the process. "I'd like to thank the Academy," he quipped, "for recognizing my talent in the category of Best Performance in a Fake News Broadcast."

The room erupted in laughter, the tension of the past few hours melting away. Tim, who had been quietly sipping his soda, spoke up. "You know, when I first joined this little rebellion, I thought you were all nuts. But now? I wouldn't want to be anywhere else."

Daniel felt a swell of pride as he looked around at his friends, his comrades in arms. They had come so far, had risked so much, and yet here they were, still standing, still fighting. It was a testament to their resilience, their unwavering commitment to the cause.

But even as they celebrated, Daniel knew that the real battle was yet to come. Brayden Funkledor was not a man to be underestimated, and he would no doubt be furious when he discovered their little stunt. They would need to be ready, to stay one step ahead, if they hoped to bring him down for good.

For now, though, Daniel allowed himself to bask in the moment, to savor the sweetness of their victory. Tomorrow would bring new challenges, new obstacles to overcome. But tonight? Tonight was for them, for the misfits and dreamers who dared to stand up against the absurdity of their world.

Professor Zander raised his glass once more, his voice ringing out clear and strong. "To the revolution, my friends. May it be as ridiculous and unpredictable as the world we live in."

And with that, they clinked their glasses, united in their mission, their laughter echoing through the night.

With the revelry winding down, the group began to disperse, each member heading off to face the uncertain future that awaited them. Alice and Kyle shared a knowing look before slipping out into the night, their fingers intertwined. Liz and Tim followed suit, their laughter echoing through the dimly lit streets as they disappeared around the corner.

Daniel, however, lingered behind, his gaze drawn to the city skyline visible through the grimy window. The neon lights of the dystopian metropolis cast an eerie glow, a kaleidoscope of colors that seemed to mock the darkness that lurked beneath the surface.

He sighed, his breath fogging up the glass. "What a fucking mess," he muttered, his voice barely audible over the distant hum of traffic.

Professor Zander clapped him on the shoulder, his eyes twinkling with mischief. "Ah, but it's our mess, isn't it? And we're going to clean it up, one ridiculous scheme at a time."

Daniel couldn't help but chuckle, the professor's enthusiasm infectious. "You really think we can do this? Take down Brayden Funkledor and his cronies?"

"Think? Dear boy, I know we can. After all, we've got something they don't."

"Oh yeah? What's that?"

"Style, of course. And a whole lot of fuck-you attitude."

Daniel shook his head, a grin spreading across his face. "You're insane, you know that?"

"Sanity is overrated, my friend. In a world gone mad, it's the crazy ones who come out on top."

With that, Professor Zander took his leave, his laughter echoing through the empty room. Daniel turned back to the window, his gaze sweeping over the city once more.

"Alright, you bastards," he whispered, his voice filled with determination. "Let's dance."

And with that, he stepped out into the night, ready to face whatever absurdity the dystopian world threw his way next. The road ahead would be long and treacherous, but for the first time in a long time, Daniel felt a sense of purpose, a glimmer of hope in the darkness.

The revolution had begun, and he would be damned if he let it fail.

The doors burst open and in marched Daniel's crew, as subtle as a demolition derby in a daycare. Alice led the charge, megaphone in hand, her grin wide enough to catch flies.

"Celery is the root of all evil!" Alice bellowed. "Down with broccoli! Asparagus for president!"

The Chuddies spun around in mass confusion, their slack-jawed stares darting between Alice and each other. Daniel scanned the room, taking in the scene. *Not a single brain cell among 'em,* he thought wryly. *This oughta be easy pickings.*

Kyle strutted out in a suit four sizes too big, the sleeves dangling past his knees. Adopting Brayden's nasally drawl, he crowed, "I'm gonna build a wall... around all the buffets! Make Obesity Great Again!"

The Chuddies erupted into guffaws, elbowing each other as they pointed at Kyle's antics. Daniel spotted Liz and Tim ducking through the distracted crowd, grim determination etched on their faces. *Good,* Daniel nodded. *Stick to the plan.*

"The only thing we have to fear is kale itself!" Alice shouted, pumping her fist.

Daniel resisted the urge to facepalm. *If the Chuddies had two synapses to rub together, they'd realize how bats—t crazy this all sounds.*

But instead, the Chuddies cheered louder, egged on by Kyle's exaggerated gesticulations. He puffed out his chest, sucked in his gut, and waddled around the stage. "We're gonna ban treadmills! And salad bars!" Kyle declared, shaking a pudgy finger at the crowd.

The Chuddies roared, a throbbing mass of ignorance. They began chanting Kyle's slogans, faces red with excitement.

Daniel allowed himself a small smirk. *Like lambs to the slaughter.* He glanced over at Alice. She flashed him a quick "ok" sign, then returned to her bizarre vegetable-themed diatribe.

So far, so good, Daniel thought. *Now let's see if Liz and Tim can get into position without these morons catching on.* He surveyed the crowd again, looking for any sign of trouble. But the Chuddies were too busy guffawing at Alice and Kyle's buffoonery to notice anything amiss.

Daniel took a deep breath, readying himself for the next phase. They'd come this far - no turning back now. Time to take down Brayden, once and for all.

Professor Zander stepped forward, a mischievous glint in his eye. With a flourish, he whipped a sheet off a jumbled contraption of wires and screens. The Chuddies fell silent, their attention drawn to the mysterious device.

"Behold!" Zander proclaimed, his voice dripping with theatrical flair. "The truth behind your beloved leader!"

He flipped a switch, and the contraption whirred to life. Holographic images flickered into existence, hovering above the Chuddies' heads. Daniel squinted, trying to make out the details.

The first image solidified, and a collective gasp rippled through the crowd. It was Brayden, caught in the act of picking his nose. And not just a subtle nostril probe - this was a full-on excavation.

"Is that-" one Chuddie stammered.

"Brayden's gold-digging expedition!" Zander crowed.

A murmur of disbelief swept through the Chuddies. Some looked away, their faces twisted with disgust. Others stared, transfixed by the grotesque spectacle.

The next hologram materialized, showing Brayden stumbling drunkenly across a stage, his combover flapping in the breeze. He lunged for the podium, missed, and face-planted into a potted fern.

"Looks like he's got a green thumb!" Zander quipped.

A few nervous titters broke out among the Chuddies. Daniel could see the cracks forming in their blind devotion.

Time to drive the point home, he thought.

Daniel strode to the front of the stage, his voice booming over the confused mutters.

"Is this the man you follow?" he challenged, gesturing to the holograms. "A bumbling buffoon who can't even navigate a simple stage?"

The Chuddies shifted uncomfortably, their eyes darting between Daniel and the embarrassing images.

"He promised you greatness," Daniel continued, his tone dripping with sarcasm. "But all he's delivered is a clown show!"

A hologram of Brayden appeared, his face contorted as he let out a resounding belch. The Chuddies cringed.

"Wake up!" Daniel implored, his voice rising with passion. "You've been duped by a charlatan! A fraud! A man who cares more about his own ego than the well-being of this nation!"

The Chuddies began to murmur among themselves, their voices tinged with doubt. Daniel could feel the tide turning.

"Brayden's policies are as ridiculous as his hairpiece!" Daniel declared, eliciting a few snickers from the crowd. "He wants to ban science! Outlaw critical thinking! Turn us all into mindless drones!"

The holograms continued to play, each one more absurd than the last. Brayden picking his teeth with a fork. Brayden tripping over his own shoelaces. Brayden accidentally setting his own toupee on fire.

"Is this the future you want?" Daniel demanded, his eyes sweeping over the sea of confused faces. "A nation led by a bumbling idiot?"

The Chuddies looked at each other, uncertainty etched on their features. Daniel could practically hear the gears turning in their heads, the first glimmers of doubt taking root.

Come on, he silently urged. *Think for yourselves for once in your lives!*

The holograms flickered and danced, a damning testament to Brayden's incompetence. And as Daniel watched, he saw the Chuddies' blind loyalty begin to crumble, replaced by the dawning realization that they'd been had.

Checkmate, Brayden, Daniel thought with grim satisfaction. *Your days of tyranny are numbered.*

Liz, a fiery redhead with a penchant for debunking conspiracy theories, found herself surrounded by a group of wide-eyed Chuddies. They clung to their absurd beliefs like life rafts in a sea of stupidity.

"Did you know that Brayden is actually a reptilian shapeshifter from the planet Zorg?" one of them whispered, his eyes darting around nervously.

Liz fought the urge to roll her eyes. "Really? I heard he was a time-traveling cyborg sent from the future to save us from ourselves."

The Chuddies gasped, their minds spinning with the possibilities. "What about the theory that he's a genetically engineered superhuman created by the Illuminati?" another piped up.

Liz couldn't help but smirk. "Oh, please. Everyone knows the Illuminati is just a front for the real masterminds: the Mole People."

The Chuddies blinked, their mouths agape. Liz could practically see the smoke billowing from their ears as they tried to process this new information.

"But... but what about the chemtrails?" a particularly dense-looking Chuddie stammered.

Liz leaned in close, her voice dropping to a conspiratorial whisper. "The chemtrails are just a distraction. The real mind control is happening through the 5G networks. Why do you think Brayden is so obsessed with his Twitter feed?"

The Chuddies murmured amongst themselves, their faces a mix of confusion and dawning horror. Liz fought back a grin, relishing in the chaos she'd sown.

These idiots are easier to manipulate than a puppet on a string, she thought with a smug sense of satisfaction.

Meanwhile, Tim, a former Chuddie himself, saw an opportunity to strike while the iron was hot. He sidled up to a small group of supporters who looked like they were starting to question their life choices.

"Listen, guys," he said, his voice low and urgent. "I know what you're going through. I drank the Kool-Aid too. But at some point, you gotta wake up and smell the bullshit."

The Chuddies looked at him warily, but Tim could see the flicker of doubt in their eyes.

"Brayden's been feeding us lies from day one," he continued, his voice growing stronger with conviction. "He's not some savior or superhero. He's just a con man with a bad haircut and an ego the size of Texas."

A few of the Chuddies nodded slowly, their expressions pensive.

"Think about it," Tim pressed on. "Has he actually done anything to make our lives better? Or has he just been lining his own pockets and stroking his own ego?"

The Chuddies shifted uncomfortably, glancing at each other with uncertainty.

Come on, you sheep, Tim thought impatiently. *Think for yourselves for once in your miserable lives.*

"It's time to take a stand," he said aloud, his voice ringing with conviction. "It's time to say enough is enough. Who's with me?"

For a moment, there was silence. Then, slowly but surely, a few hands began to rise. A ripple of doubt spread through the crowd, growing stronger with each passing second.

Gotcha, Tim thought with a triumphant grin. *The seeds of rebellion have been planted. Now let's watch them grow.*

Brayden waddled onto the stage, his combover flapping in the breeze like a half-dead squirrel clinging to a tree branch. He smiled that stupid, self-satisfied smile, completely oblivious to the chaos unfolding around him.

"My fellow Chuddies!" he bellowed, his voice dripping with false bravado. "Don't listen to these losers and haters! They're just jealous of our tremendous success!"

But his words were drowned out by a cacophony of laughter and jeers. The Chuddies, who had once hung on his every word, were now looking at him with a mix of confusion and disdain.

Look at him, Daniel thought, watching Brayden flounder on stage. *He's like a fat, orange penguin trying to tap dance.*

Brayden, undeterred, launched into one of his trademark nonsensical rants. "We're going to build a wall around the moon, and we're going to make the Martians pay for it!" he declared, his face turning an alarming shade of red.

The crowd erupted into laughter, and Daniel saw his chance. He nodded to his group, and they sprang into action.

Alice stepped forward, wearing a blond wig and an oversized suit. "I'm Brayden, and I approve this message!" she said, mimicking his voice with eerie accuracy. "I promise to make America grate again, one block of cheese at a time!"

The Chuddies howled with laughter as Alice launched into a series of increasingly absurd impressions, each one highlighting one of Brayden's most infamous blunders.

Next up was Kyle, who strutted onto the stage wearing a diaper and a "Make America Grate Again" hat. "I'm not a baby!" he whined, stomping his feet. "I'm a very stable genius!"

The crowd roared with laughter as Kyle proceeded to throw a tantrum, pounding his fists on the ground and wailing about fake news and witch hunts.

They're eating it up, Daniel thought, watching the Chuddies' faces. *They're actually starting to see how ridiculous this all is.*

As the skits continued, Daniel could see the doubt and confusion growing on the faces of the Chuddies. They were caught between their loyalty to Brayden and the undeniable absurdity of his reign.

Come on, he thought, silently urging them on. *You're almost there. Just a little further.*

Brayden, meanwhile, was turning an alarming shade of purple, his combover now completely askew. He sputtered and stammered, trying desperately to regain control of the situation.

But it was too late. The tide had turned, and the Chuddies were beginning to see the truth. They looked at Brayden with new eyes, seeing him for the blustering, incompetent fool he really was.

We did it, Daniel thought, feeling a surge of triumph. *We actually did it.*

Professor Zander, sensing the moment was ripe, stepped forward with a flourish. "Ladies and gentlemen," he announced, his voice booming over the din, "I present to you the latest breaking news from the Brayden administration!"

With a dramatic gesture, he activated a holographic projection that filled the air above the stage. The Chuddies gasped as a familiar figure appeared: Brayden himself, seated at his desk in the Oval Office.

"My fellow Americhuds," the holographic Brayden began, his voice a perfect imitation of the real thing, "I come to you today with grave news. It seems that the forces of logic and reason have infiltrated our great nation, threatening to destroy everything we hold dear."

The Chuddies murmured in confusion, unsure of what to make of this unexpected development. The holographic Brayden continued, his face contorting into a grotesque caricature of concern.

"But fear not, my loyal supporters! I have a plan to combat this insidious threat. From this day forward, all citizens will be required to wear tin foil hats to protect against the insidious rays of common sense!"

The crowd erupted into a mix of laughter and disbelief. The absurdity of the situation was finally sinking in, and even the most ardent Chuddies were beginning to question their allegiance.

This is it, Daniel thought, his heart pounding with excitement. *We've got them right where we want them.*

As if on cue, Alice leaped onto the stage, megaphone in hand. "Attention, Chuddies!" she bellowed, her voice cutting through the chaos. "Repeat after me: Brayden is a fraud! Brayden is a fraud!"

To Daniel's amazement, the chant began to spread through the crowd, growing louder and more insistent with each repetition. The Chuddies, caught up in the moment, joined in with gusto, their voices rising in a cacophony of mockery and defiance.

I can't believe it, Daniel thought, watching the scene unfold with a sense of awe. *We actually pulled it off. We're going to bring down Brayden once and for all.*

Brayden, his combover flapping in the breeze, stared out at the sea of chanting faces with a mixture of disbelief and desperation. His tiny hands clenched into fists as he stepped forward, his voice straining to be heard above the din.

"My fellow Chuddies!" he cried, his eyes bulging with barely contained rage. "I implore you, do not be swayed by these... these charlatans! They seek to undermine the very fabric of our society, to tear down the walls of ignorance and blind loyalty that we have worked so hard to build!"

But his words were lost in the tumult, drowned out by the relentless chanting and the occasional burst of laughter. Daniel, seizing the moment, leaped onto the stage beside Alice, his voice booming with a mix of triumph and incredulity.

"Look around you, Brayden!" he shouted, gesturing to the crowd. "Your reign of stupidity is coming to an end. The people have finally seen through your lies and your cheap tricks. They're ready for change, and there's nothing you can do to stop it!"

Brayden sputtered and fumed, his face turning a mottled shade of purple. "You... you'll pay for this!" he screamed, his voice cracking with impotent rage. "I'll have you all thrown in the dungeons! I'll... I'll..."

But his threats were met with nothing but laughter and jeers. The Chuddies, emboldened by Daniel's words, surged forward, their chants growing louder and more insistent.

This is really happening, Daniel thought, his heart swelling with a sense of pride and purpose. *We're actually making a difference. We're actually changing things.*

He turned to Alice, a grin spreading across his face. "You ready for this?" he asked, his voice barely audible above the roar of the crowd.

Alice nodded, her eyes sparkling with mischief. "Let's do it," she said, raising her megaphone to her lips.

Together, they faced the crowd, their voices rising in unison. "People of Chuddington!" they cried, their words echoing across the square. "The time has come to take back our country, to cast off the shackles of ignorance and stupidity! Are you with us?"

The answering roar was deafening, a tidal wave of sound that swept across the square and beyond. In that moment, Daniel knew that they had won, that the tide had finally turned in their favor.

And to think, he mused, a wry smile tugging at the corners of his mouth, *it all started with a few cheap laughs and a holographic combover.*

As the crowd's cheers reached a crescendo, a sudden hush fell over the square. All eyes turned to the far end of the stage, where a group of figures emerged from the shadows. It was the rogue scientists, their lab coats billowing in the breeze, their faces etched with determination.

Professor Zander stepped forward, his voice booming through the speakers. "People of Chuddington, we have something to show you. Something that will change everything you thought you knew about this presidency, about this entire regime."

With a flourish, he pressed a button on a small device in his hand. A holographic screen flickered to life above the stage, casting an eerie glow over the transfixed crowd.

No way, Daniel thought, his eyes widening in disbelief. *They're actually going through with it. They're really gonna expose the whole damn thing.*

The screen flashed with a series of images, each more damning than the last. Secret documents, hidden camera footage, audio recordings of Brayden's most incriminating moments. The evidence was irrefutable, painting a picture of a presidency built on lies, manipulation, and an elaborate social experiment designed to test the limits of human gullibility.

The Chuddies stood in stunned silence, their mouths agape, their eyes glued to the screen. Daniel could see the realization dawning on their faces, the slow, painful process of understanding just how thoroughly they'd been duped.

And then, like a dam bursting, the crowd erupted. Shouts of outrage mingled with peals of laughter, as the absurdity of the situation finally sank in. They had been played for fools, but now, armed with the truth, they were finally free.

Daniel turned to his friends, his chest swelling with a sense of triumph. "We did it," he said, his voice barely audible above the din. "We actually fucking did it."

Alice grinned, her megaphone still clutched in her hand. "Was there ever any doubt?" she asked, her voice tinged with sarcasm.

Kyle, his oversized suit now rumpled and stained with sweat, clapped Daniel on the back. "Dude, that was epic. Like, I think I peed a little, but it was totally worth it."

Liz and Tim, their faces flushed with excitement, joined in the laughter. For a moment, they all basked in the chaotic triumph of their absurdly orchestrated showdown, savoring the sweet taste of victory.

And to think, Daniel mused, his eyes scanning the jubilant crowd, *all it took was a little bit of humor, a dash of courage, and a whole lot of fuck-you attitude.*

He smiled, knowing that this was just the beginning. There was still work to be done, a country to rebuild, a new future to shape. But for now, in this moment of liberation and laughter, anything seemed possible.

As the laughter and chaos began to subside, Daniel and his band of misfits knew it was time to make their exit. They had accomplished what they set out to do, but lingering too long could invite unwanted attention from the remnants of Brayden's loyal followers.

"Alright, gang," Daniel said, his voice low and conspiratorial. "Let's blow this popsicle stand before the Chuddies regroup and start asking questions."

Professor Zander, still giddy from the success of his holographic exposé, nodded in agreement. "Yes, yes, we must retreat to plan our next move. The revolution may have begun, but there's still much work to be done."

The group began to weave their way through the crowd, dodging the occasional Chuddie who seemed to be snapping out of their stupor. Liz, ever the quick-witted one, couldn't resist throwing out a few more conspiracy theories as they went.

"Hey, did you hear about the secret underground bunker where they're keeping all the confiscated sense of humor?" she asked, eliciting a few chuckles from her friends.

As they reached the edge of the crowd, Daniel paused for a moment, turning to take one last look at the scene they were leaving behind. The Chuddies, once a formidable force of blind loyalty, now seemed lost and confused, like puppets whose strings had been cut.

This is just the beginning, Daniel thought, a sense of determination washing over him. *We've shown them the truth, but now it's up to them to do something with it.*

With a nod to his friends, Daniel led the way out of the square, their footsteps echoing against the pavement. The air around them crackled with energy, a tangible sense of change that seemed to permeate every molecule.

"So, what now?" Tim asked, his voice a mix of excitement and uncertainty.

Daniel grinned, a mischievous glint in his eye. "Now, my friends, we regroup, we plan, and we keep fighting. Because if there's one thing I've learned, it's that laughter is the most powerful weapon we have against tyranny and stupidity."

As they disappeared into the city streets, the weight of their accomplishment began to sink in. They had done the impossible, had shattered the illusion that had held a nation captive. And while the road ahead was sure to be filled with challenges and obstacles, they knew that they had the strength, the wit, and the audacity to face whatever came their way.

The revolution of laughter has begun, Daniel mused, a smile playing at the corners of his mouth. *And God help anyone who tries to stand in our way.*

Daniel's palms were slick with sweat as he gripped the podium, his knuckles white as bleached bones. The makeshift stage creaked beneath his feet, a ramshackle soapbox thrown together with spare plywood and rusty nails. Out in the restless crowd, skeptical eyes pinned him like darts on a corkboard. Chuddies in their garish purple robes milled about, muttering prayers to the great god Brayden. And the merely curious gawked like yokels at a carnival freak show, wide-eyed and slack-jawed.

"Well, shit," Daniel mumbled under his breath. His heart jackhammered against his ribcage as if trying to punch its way out. He imagined it bursting free, bouncing off the stage and into the churning sea of faces. Would serve them right, he thought, the ungrateful bastards.

With a deep breath that did jack all to calm his nerves, Daniel shuffled to the edge of the stage. He gripped the mic in a sweaty fist.

"So, uh, I'm Daniel," he started, his voice cracking like a prepubescent choir boy. "Though most of you probably know me as that guy who couldn't lead a pack of lemmings off a cliff."

A wave of snickers rippled through the crowd. Daniel felt a flicker of relief. At least they weren't bombarding him with rotten fruit. Yet.

He cleared his throat and soldiered on. "Seriously though, I'm not gonna stand up here and pretend I'm some great revolutionary leader. Hell, I can barely lead myself to the bathroom most mornings." More chuckles from the peanut gallery.

As Daniel spoke, his eyes scanned the multicolored patchwork of faces. Anger simmered in some eyes, boredom glazed others. He spotted a few allies in the mix - Alice with her quirked brow and encouraging nod, Kyle flashing an ironic devil-horns gesture. Good old friends, loyal to the bitter end. Crazy bastards.

Behind the podium, Daniel's free hand clenched into a fist, blunt nails digging into his palm. This is it, he told himself. The make or break moment. Time to yank back the curtain on this whole rotten circus. He just prayed he wouldn't projectile vomit in the process.

Daniel took a breath and launched into his tirade, his voice gaining strength with each word.

"Now, I know you're all here because you're fed up with the way things are. And who can blame you? I mean, have you seen the state of this country lately? It's like a bad acid trip without the fun hallucinations."

He began to pace the stage, his hands slicing through the air as he spoke. "And at the center of this psychedelic nightmare is our esteemed leader, President Brayden. A man so dense, light bends around him. A man who thinks 'foreign policy' is deciding which country to order takeout from."

Laughter began to build, nervous at first, then growing bolder. Daniel felt a surge of adrenaline, his heart pounding in time with the crowd's energy.

"But here's the real kicker," he continued, his voice dripping with sarcasm. "Brayden's not just a bumbling idiot. No, no, that would be too easy. He's a bumbling idiot with power. And he's using that power to turn this country into his own personal playground."

Daniel launched into a series of increasingly absurd examples, each one more ridiculous than the last. Brayden's plan to combat climate change by outlawing ice cream. His proposal to solve the housing crisis by building a giant bouncy castle for the homeless. His idea to boost the economy by replacing currency with Monopoly money.

As he spoke, Daniel watched the Chuddies in the crowd, their expressions shifting from stony-faced disapproval to reluctant amusement. A few even cracked smiles, their rigid postures loosening as they leaned in to listen.

"You see?" Daniel cried, his voice rising to a fever pitch. "This is what we're dealing with, people. A leader so disconnected from reality, he makes the Mad Hatter look like a paragon of sanity. And we're all just sitting back and letting it happen, like a bunch of lobotomized lemmings."

From the sidelines, Alice and Kyle cheered, their voices rising above the din. "Tell it like it is, Daniel!" Alice shouted, her fist pumping the air. Kyle let out a whoop of agreement, his grin stretching from ear to ear.

Daniel felt a rush of gratitude for his friends, their support fueling his momentum. He turned back to the crowd, his eyes blazing with determination.

"But here's the thing," he said, his voice dropping to a conspiratorial whisper. "We don't have to take this lying down. We have the power to change things, to take back control from the lunatics running the asylum."

He paused for effect, letting his words sink in. The crowd leaned forward, hanging on his every word.

"So what do you say?" Daniel asked, his voice rising to a crescendo. "Are you ready to join the resistance? Are you ready to fight back against the absurdity and take a stand for sanity?"

The crowd erupted in cheers, their voices merging into a deafening roar. Daniel felt a surge of triumph, his heart swelling with pride. He caught Alice's eye across the stage, her grin mirroring his own.

For a moment, anything seemed possible. The future was theirs for the taking, and Daniel was ready to lead the charge.

Little did he know, the biggest twist was yet to come...

Just as Daniel basked in the crowd's adulation, the sound of flapping fabric caught his attention. He spun around, his jaw dropping as a group of rogue scientists burst onto the stage, their pristine lab coats billowing behind them like superhero capes. The crowd fell silent, their eyes widening at the unexpected interruption.

The lead scientist, a wiry man with an unruly mop of hair and a manic gleam in his eyes, strutted up to Daniel, his grin bordering on the unhinged. Without warning, he snatched the microphone from Daniel's hand with a flourish, his movements as exaggerated as a vaudeville performer.

"Thank you, thank you," the scientist said, bowing deeply to the stunned audience. "But I'm afraid we have some news that will blow your minds more than any of Daniel's witty one-liners."

Daniel stepped back, his brow furrowing in confusion. What the hell was going on? He glanced at Alice and Kyle, who looked equally perplexed.

The scientist cleared his throat, his grin widening. "Ladies and gentlemen, we have a confession to make. Brayden's presidency, this entire dystopian nightmare you've been living in... it's all been one big, elaborate social experiment!"

The crowd gasped in unison, their shock palpable. Daniel felt his own jaw drop, his mind reeling. A social experiment? What the actual fuck?

"That's right," the scientist continued, his voice rising with barely contained glee. "We wanted to see just how far we could push the boundaries of absurdity before you all caught on. And let me tell you, it's been one wild ride!"

Daniel shook his head, trying to process the revelation. He'd always known Brayden's presidency was a farce, but this? This was a whole new level of insanity.

The scientist cackled, his laughter bordering on maniacal. "But don't worry, folks. The experiment is over now. You can all go back to your regularly scheduled programming of mediocrity and monotony."

As the crowd erupted in a mixture of outrage and disbelief, Daniel couldn't help but feel a twinge of admiration for the audacity of it all. In a world where nothing made sense, the idea of a social experiment seemed almost fitting.

He glanced at Alice and Kyle, a wry grin tugging at his lips. "Well, shit," he muttered. "Guess we've been punk'd on a cosmic scale."

Alice rolled her eyes, but Daniel could see the hint of a smile playing at the corners of her mouth. "Leave it to you to find the humor in this mess," she said.

Kyle shook his head, his expression caught between amusement and exasperation. "I swear, man, our lives are one big, cosmic joke."

As the scientists continued their bombshell announcement, Daniel couldn't help but feel a sense of relief wash over him. Maybe, just maybe, this was the wake-up call the world needed to snap out of its collective insanity.

Or maybe, he thought with a snort, it was just another twist in the never-ending circus of absurdity that was his life. Either way, he was ready to embrace the chaos and see where it led him next.

Daniel watched as the Chuddies, their faces contorted with rage, surged forward, their fists raised in defiance. "You lied to us!" they shouted, their voices blending into a discordant chorus. "We trusted you!"

The scientists, to their credit, stood their ground, their expressions a mix of determination and barely concealed glee. "The truth hurts, doesn't it?" the lead scientist called out, his voice cutting through the din. "But sometimes, the only way to wake people up is to give them a good, hard slap in the face."

Daniel couldn't help but chuckle at the sheer audacity of it all. He leaned over to Alice, his voice low and conspiratorial. "You know, I almost feel bad for the Chuddies. They've been living in a fantasy world for so long, they don't know how to handle reality."

Alice snorted, her eyes never leaving the chaos unfolding before them. "Reality? What's that? I thought we were all just living in one big, twisted simulation."

"Maybe we are," Kyle chimed in, his voice tinged with amusement. "And maybe this is just the glitch in the matrix we've been waiting for."

As the Chuddies continued their angry tirade, Daniel couldn't help but feel a sense of detachment from it all. It was as if he was watching a movie, a surreal and slightly ridiculous one at that.

But then again, he thought, what part of his life wasn't surreal and ridiculous these days? In a world where a talking baboon could become president and scientists could treat the entire population like lab rats, nothing seemed too far-fetched anymore.

He glanced at his friends, a sudden wave of affection washing over him. "You know what? Fuck it. If this is all just some cosmic joke, we might as well enjoy the punchline."

And with that, he turned his attention back to the stage, ready to embrace whatever twisted plot twist the universe had in store for them next.

Brayden, his face a study in bewilderment and indignation, stumbled forward, pushing his way through the seething crowd. His beady eyes darted left and right, as if searching for a friendly face amidst the sea of anger and betrayal.

"Now, now, let's all just calm down," he blustered, his voice cracking under the strain. "This is all just a big misunderstanding. I'm sure if we sit down and talk this through, we can sort everything out."

But his words were lost in the uproar, drowned out by the shouts and jeers of the Chuddies. They surged forward, their faces contorted with rage, their fists pumping the air in a frenzied display of outrage.

Brayden's eyes widened in panic as he realized the futility of his efforts. He opened his mouth to speak again, but all that came out was a series of nonsensical phrases, snippets of his campaign slogans jumbled together in a desperate attempt to regain control.

"Make America Chud again! No more fake news! I'm the best president, the very best, everyone says so!"

But his words only served to fuel the flames of anger, and the crowd pressed in closer, their breath hot on his face, their eyes blazing with a fury that couldn't be quenched.

In the midst of the chaos, the scientists stood tall and unruffled, their voices cutting through the din like a beacon of reason. They held up charts and graphs, their data laid out in stark black and white, a damning indictment of Brayden's presidency.

"As you can see," the lead scientist said, his voice calm and measured, "the data speaks for itself. Brayden's policies have been a complete failure, a mockery of leadership and a testament to the dangers of ignorance and incompetence."

He pointed to a particularly damning chart, his finger tracing the plummeting lines of approval ratings and economic indicators. "This experiment has shown us the true cost of electing a leader based on populist rhetoric and empty promises. It's time for us to wake up and face the reality of our situation."

The crowd fell silent for a moment, their anger momentarily replaced by a sense of stunned realization. They looked at the charts and graphs, their eyes widening as the truth sank in.

Daniel watched the scene unfold, his heart racing with a mix of excitement and trepidation. He knew that this was a pivotal moment, a turning point in the battle against ignorance and absurdity.

He leaned in closer to Alice and Kyle, his voice low and urgent. "This is it, guys. This is our chance to make a difference, to show the world what happens when you let a baboon run the show."

Alice nodded, her eyes sparkling with determination. "Let's do this. Let's take back our country from the Chuddies and their orange overlord."

Kyle grinned, his fist pumping the air in a gesture of solidarity. "Fuck yeah! It's time for a revolution, baby. A revolution of reason and common sense."

And with that, they turned their attention back to the stage, ready to join the fray and fight for the future they believed in.

Daniel seized the moment, leaping onto the stage with a newfound vigor. He grabbed the microphone, his voice booming across the restless crowd. "Listen up, folks! We've all been played for fools, but it's time to take back control!"

The audience roared in agreement, their fists pumping the air as Daniel's words ignited a fire within them. He continued, his tone fierce and unapologetic. "We can't let this absurdity go on any longer. It's time to reject the ignorance that allowed Brayden to rise to power. It's time to embrace the lessons we've learned and fight for a future that makes sense!"

The crowd's anger reached a fever pitch, their voices rising in a cacophony of outrage and determination. They chanted in unison, "No more Brayden! No more lies! We demand the truth, and we demand it now!"

Daniel's heart swelled with pride as he watched the tide of public opinion turn before his eyes. He stepped back, his chest heaving with the adrenaline of the moment. "This is our time, people! This is our chance to make a difference!"

The chanting grew louder, the crowd's energy palpable as they rallied behind Daniel's words. "Down with Brayden! Up with reason!" they shouted, their voices merging into a powerful chorus.

Alice and Kyle rushed to Daniel's side, their faces beaming with excitement. "You did it, man!" Kyle exclaimed, clapping Daniel on the back. "You've got them eating out of the palm of your hand."

Alice nodded, her eyes shining with admiration. "This is just the beginning. We're going to take this momentum and run with it, all the way to the fucking White House if we have to."

Daniel grinned, his heart racing with the thrill of victory. He looked out at the sea of faces, each one a reflection of the hope and determination that now coursed through his veins. "Buckle up, Brayden," he muttered under his breath. "Your days of bullshit are officially numbered."

Amidst the chaos, the scientists quietly slipped away, their mission complete. They disappeared into the shadows, leaving behind a crowd that buzzed with a mix of bewilderment and enlightenment. The experiment had achieved its unexpected conclusion, and the aftermath was a sight to behold.

Daniel scanned the crowd, his eyes wide with disbelief. "Holy shit, did that just happen?" he muttered to himself, running a hand through his disheveled hair. The adrenaline still pumped through his veins, making him feel like he could take on the world.

As the dust settled, Daniel and his friends regrouped, their faces alight with the thrill of victory. Alice bounded over to him, her eyes sparkling with mischief. "That was fucking brilliant, Daniel!" she exclaimed, throwing her arms around him in a fierce hug.

Kyle joined in, his grin stretching from ear to ear. "Dude, you were on fire up there! I've never seen anything like it."

Daniel laughed, the sound a mix of relief and pure joy. "I can't believe we actually pulled this off. It's like a goddamn miracle."

"A miracle of science, maybe," Alice quipped, her eyebrow arched in amusement. "Who knew those lab coats could cause such a stir?"

The three friends exchanged high-fives and hugs, their camaraderie strengthened by the absurdity of their shared experience. They had taken on the impossible and won, and the feeling was nothing short of euphoric.

"So, what now?" Kyle asked, his eyes darting between Daniel and Alice. "We can't just let this momentum go to waste."

Daniel nodded, his mind already racing with possibilities. "We keep pushing, that's what. We take this energy and we channel it into something bigger, something that can't be ignored."

Alice grinned, her expression fierce with determination. "I'm with you, Daniel. Let's show these bastards what happens when you mess with the wrong people."

As the trio stood there, surrounded by the buzzing crowd, they knew that this was just the beginning. They had sparked a revolution, and there was no turning back now. The future was theirs for the taking, and they were ready to fight for it, no matter what the cost.

The sun began to set on the chaotic scene, casting an otherworldly glow over the makeshift stage and the sea of faces. Daniel, Alice, and

Kyle stood together, their silhouettes illuminated by the fading light, a united front against the uncertainty that lay ahead.

Daniel's mind raced with the possibilities, the weight of their achievement slowly sinking in. They had exposed the truth, shattered the illusion of Brayden's presidency, but what would come next? Would the people rise up and demand change, or would they slip back into complacency, content with the status quo?

"We can't let this fire die out," Daniel said, his voice low and intense. "We've got to keep pushing, keep fighting. This is just the beginning."

Alice nodded, her eyes blazing with the same fierce determination. "We've got to organize, mobilize. We need to reach out to every corner of this godforsaken country and make sure everyone knows what happened here today."

Kyle, his usual jovial demeanor replaced by a serious intensity, chimed in. "We need a plan, a strategy. We can't just wing it and hope for the best. We've got to be smart about this."

The three friends huddled together, their heads bowed in deep discussion. They traded ideas back and forth, their words tumbling over each other in a frenzied rush of inspiration. They knew they had a long road ahead of them, but they were ready to face whatever challenges lay in wait.

As the last rays of sunlight faded from the sky, Daniel, Alice, and Kyle emerged from their huddle, their faces set with grim determination. They had a plan, a course of action that would take them to the heart of the corrupt system they sought to overthrow.

With one last look at the dispersing crowd, the trio set off into the gathering darkness, their footsteps echoing with the weight of their purpose. The future was unwritten, but they were ready to be the authors of their own destiny. Come what may, they would face it together, united in their quest for truth and justice in a world gone mad.

Daniel blinked in disbelief as the crowd around him erupted into a deafening roar of cheers and shouts. He glanced at his friends Kyle and Alice, their faces mirroring his own dumbfounded expression. They had actually done it - defeated the nefarious Brayden Funkledor and his absurd schemes. It seemed too good to be true.

A group of rogue scientists wearing lab coats covered in silly equations appeared, roughly seizing Brayden by the arms. "Unhand me, you traitorous twits!" Brayden screeched as they hauled him away. "This isn't over! I'll be back to establish a new world order of mandatory mirth and merriment!"

His protests were drowned out by the crowd's uproarious laughter and jeers. Brayden tried to wrench himself free, only to trip over his own feet and faceplant on the ground in a undignified heap. "Oopsie doodle!" he yelped as the scientists dragged him back up.

Daniel couldn't help but chuckle at the ridiculous scene unfolding before him. After all the chaos and craziness Brayden had put them through, it was immensely satisfying to see him get his comical comeuppance.

"Smell ya later, Funkledork!" someone in the crowd shouted gleefully. The rest of the onlookers erupted into raucous laughter and started chanting "Funkledork! Funkledork!" as Brayden was unceremoniously hauled out of sight, still yelling nonsense.

Holy shit, we actually pulled it off, Daniel thought, shaking his head in amazement. He caught Kyle's eye and they both burst out laughing at the same time, the reality of their triumph finally sinking in.

As the laughter died down, the crowd's attention shifted to Daniel. Whispers rippled through the throng, growing louder and more excited. "That's him! The guy who stopped Brayden!" someone shouted.

Suddenly, the crowd erupted into chants of "Daniel! Daniel! Daniel!"

Daniel froze, his eyes widening in surprise. "Oh, crap," he muttered under his breath. He glanced around awkwardly, unsure how to react to the unexpected attention.

Alice nudged him with her elbow, a smirk playing on her lips. "Well, well, well. Look who's the big hero now," she teased.

"Shut up," Daniel mumbled, feeling his face heat up. He rubbed the back of his neck, a hesitant grin tugging at the corners of his mouth.

Kyle slung an arm around Daniel's shoulders, grinning from ear to ear. "Dude, you're like, famous now! Bask in the glory, man!"

"I mean, we all did it together," Daniel said, trying to downplay his role. But he couldn't deny the warm swell of pride in his chest as he looked out at the cheering crowd.

Alice rolled her eyes. "Oh, don't be so modest. You're the one who came up with the plan."

"Yeah, and nearly got us all killed in the process," Kyle added with a snort.

Daniel elbowed him in the ribs. "Hey, it worked, didn't it?"

As the three friends bantered back and forth, the surreal nature of the situation started to sink in. Here they were, a bunch of misfits who had somehow managed to take down a tyrannical dictator and save the world from a lifetime of forced fun.

"Is this really happening?" Alice asked, shaking her head in disbelief.

"Pinch me, I must be dreaming," Kyle quipped.

Daniel laughed, feeling a surge of camaraderie with his friends. They had been through hell together, but they had come out on the other side stronger than ever.

The crowd continued to chant Daniel's name, their voices growing louder and more insistent. He looked at Alice and Kyle, a mischievous glint in his eye.

"Shall we give the people what they want?" he asked, raising an eyebrow.

Alice grinned. "Lead the way, hero."

With that, Daniel took a deep breath and stepped forward, ready to face the adoring masses. It was time to embrace his newfound status as the unlikely savior of the world, and he was going to do it with his best friends by his side.

Overzealous supporters swarmed around Daniel, Alice, and Kyle, their faces lit up with manic grins. A middle-aged woman wearing a neon-pink wig thrust a pen and a tattered piece of paper into Daniel's face. "Can I get your autograph, please? You're my hero!" she gushed, bouncing on her toes.

Daniel blinked, taken aback by the woman's enthusiasm. "Uh, sure," he mumbled, scribbling his name on the paper.

Next to him, Kyle was accosted by a group of teenage girls, their phones held high as they struck ridiculous poses. "Selfie time!" they squealed, draping themselves over Kyle like a human cape.

Alice snickered as she watched Kyle's discomfort. "Smile for the camera, pretty boy," she teased, earning herself a withering glare.

The absurdity of the situation was not lost on Daniel. Just yesterday, they were nobodies, scraping by in a world gone mad. Now, they were being treated like celebrities, their every move watched and admired.

As the crowd's fervor reached a fever pitch, a makeshift stage appeared out of nowhere, hastily constructed from discarded crates and planks. "Speech! Speech!" the crowd chanted, pushing Daniel towards the stage.

He looked back at his friends, panic rising in his throat. "I can't do this," he hissed, his palms sweating.

Alice and Kyle exchanged a glance, their eyes glinting with mischief. "Oh, yes, you can," Alice said, giving Daniel a shove. "Get up there and give 'em hell, hero."

Kyle nodded, a smirk playing on his lips. "You got this, man. Just pretend you're talking to us."

With exaggerated gestures and mock encouragement, they propelled Daniel onto the stage. He stumbled, nearly falling on his face, but managed to catch himself at the last moment.

The crowd roared as he straightened up, their faces a sea of expectant grins. Daniel's mind raced, trying to find the right words. He glanced back at Alice and Kyle, who were now making goofy faces and giving him exaggerated thumbs-up signs.

"You got this, Danny-boy!" Kyle called out, his voice dripping with sarcasm.

Daniel shook his head, a reluctant grin tugging at his lips. Leave it to his friends to make a mockery of the most important moment of his life.

He turned back to the crowd, taking a deep breath. It was now or never. He had to say something, even if it meant making a complete fool of himself.

Here goes nothing, he thought, stepping up to the edge of the stage. *Time to embrace the chaos and give the performance of a lifetime.*

Daniel cleared his throat, the sound echoing through the expectant silence. "Well, folks, I never thought I'd be standing here, giving a speech after the wild ride we've been on." He paused, his eyes scanning the sea of faces. "But then again, I never thought I'd be part of a ragtag group of misfits taking down a megalomaniac like Brayden Funkledor either."

The crowd erupted in laughter and cheers, their energy palpable. Daniel grinned, feeling a surge of confidence. "You know, when we started this journey, we had no idea what we were getting into. We were just a bunch of regular people, trying to survive in this crazy, messed-up world. But somehow, along the way, we found ourselves in the middle of a revolution."

He shook his head, chuckling at the absurdity of it all. "I mean, who would've thought that a group of nobodies like us could bring down a guy like Brayden? It's like a bad joke, isn't it? The punchline being that we actually succeeded!"

The crowd roared with laughter, their faces alight with amusement and relief. Daniel could see the weight lifting off their shoulders, the realization that they were finally free from Brayden's tyranny.

"But you know what the real kicker is?" Daniel continued, his tone growing more serious. "It's that we didn't do it alone. We had help from the most unlikely places. From the rogue scientists who saw through Brayden's lies, to the everyday people who risked everything to support us. This victory belongs to all of us."

As he spoke, Daniel could see the crowd nodding in agreement, their expressions a mix of pride and gratitude. They had all played a part in this revolution, no matter how small.

"So, let's take a moment to appreciate the sheer ridiculousness of our situation," Daniel said, a grin spreading across his face. "We're a bunch of misfits, standing here in the ruins of a society that was built on lies and manipulation. But you know what? We're still standing. We're still laughing. And that, my friends, is the biggest 'fuck you' we could ever give to Brayden and his cronies."

The crowd erupted in a deafening cheer, their voices rising in a cacophony of joy and defiance. Daniel could feel the energy coursing through him, the sense of unity and purpose that had brought them all together.

As he stepped back from the edge of the stage, he caught sight of Alice and Kyle, their faces split in wide grins. They rushed forward, enveloping him in a tight hug.

"Dude, that was awesome!" Kyle exclaimed, slapping him on the back. "You had them eating out of the palm of your hand!"

Alice nodded, her eyes shining with pride. "You nailed it, Daniel. You really nailed it."

Daniel grinned, feeling a warmth spreading through his chest. He knew that this was just the beginning, that there would be more challenges and obstacles to come. But for now, in this moment, he was content to bask in the glow of their victory, to revel in the absurdity and wonder of it all.

We did it, he thought, looking out at the cheering crowd. *We actually did it. And damn, if it doesn't feel good.*

As the cheers began to subside, a group of rogue scientists stepped onto the stage, their lab coats fluttering in the breeze. Dr. Eliza Hoffman, a tall woman with a shock of frizzy red hair, stepped forward, her eyes twinkling with mischief.

"Ladies and gentlemen," she began, her voice amplified by the microphone, "we have a confession to make. This entire debacle, from the rise of Brayden Funkledor to the heroic actions of Daniel and his friends, was part of a grand social experiment."

The crowd fell silent, their mouths agape. Daniel exchanged a bewildered glance with Alice and Kyle, who looked equally stunned.

Dr. Hoffman continued, her tone laced with barely contained glee. "You see, we wanted to test the limits of human gullibility, to see how far we could push the boundaries of absurdity before people would start to question the status quo. And boy, did you all deliver!"

She gestured to a screen behind her, which flickered to life with a series of graphs and charts. "As you can see here, our carefully calculated algorithms predicted that society would reach peak ridiculousness around the time of Brayden's rise to power. And thanks to our intrepid heroes," she nodded towards Daniel and his friends, "we were able to prove our hypothesis correct."

The crowd murmured, a mix of confusion and amusement rippling through their ranks. Dr. Hoffman's colleagues, Dr. Rajesh Patel and Dr. Mei Ling, stepped forward, their expressions a mix of academic fascination and barely suppressed laughter.

"Of course, we never meant for things to get quite so out of hand," Dr. Patel admitted, his eyes crinkling behind his thick-rimmed glasses.

"But you know what they say about the best-laid plans of mice and scientists..."

Dr. Mei Ling nodded sagely, her sleek black ponytail bobbing. "Indeed. We may have unleashed a bit of chaos, but in doing so, we also revealed the incredible resilience and adaptability of the human spirit. Even in the face of utter nonsense, you all found a way to band together and fight back."

The crowd's reaction was a mix of shock, disbelief, and grudging amusement. Some shook their heads in wonder, while others burst into laughter, the absurdity of the situation finally sinking in.

Daniel couldn't help but chuckle, the tension draining from his body. He looked at Alice and Kyle, who were grinning like idiots, their eyes sparkling with mirth.

"Can you believe this shit?" Kyle asked, shaking his head. "We've been part of some twisted science fair project all along."

Alice snorted, punching him lightly on the arm. "Hey, at least we got to be the stars of the show. And who knows? Maybe this whole thing will end up in some psychology textbook someday."

Daniel smiled, feeling a sense of camaraderie and shared experience with the crowd around him. They had all been through something strange and wonderful together, and somehow, that made everything seem a little bit brighter.

We may be living in a world gone mad, he thought, *but at least we're in it together. And if laughter really is the best medicine, then we've got one hell of a prescription.*

As Daniel and his friends descended from the stage, they were immediately engulfed by a throng of well-wishers and curious onlookers. Hands reached out to pat them on the back, and voices clamored for their attention.

"Dude, that was epic!" a young man in a neon green hoodie exclaimed, grinning from ear to ear. "You guys are like, the heroes of the revolution or something."

Daniel laughed, high-fiving the enthusiastic supporter. "I don't know about heroes, but we definitely gave Brayden a run for his money."

"Can I get a selfie with you?" a girl with bright purple hair asked, her eyes wide with excitement. "I want to prove to my friends that I met the legendary troublemakers in person."

Alice smirked, striking an exaggerated pose. "Sure thing, but make sure you get my good side. I've got a reputation to uphold."

As the group posed for photos and answered questions, Kyle leaned in close to Daniel, his voice low and conspiratorial. "Is it just me, or does this feel like some kind of bizarre dream? I keep waiting for someone to pinch me and wake me up."

Daniel nodded, his eyes scanning the crowd. "I know what you mean. It's like we've stepped into an alternate reality where anything is possible, and the rules don't apply anymore."

"Speaking of rules," Alice chimed in, her eyes sparkling with mischief, "remember that time we infiltrated Brayden's secret lair? I thought for sure we were going to end up in some kind of dystopian prison."

Kyle snorted, shaking his head. "Yeah, and then Daniel had the brilliant idea to disguise ourselves as maintenance workers. I've never seen someone look so ridiculous in a jumpsuit."

"Hey, it worked, didn't it?" Daniel retorted, grinning. "And let's not forget about the time we hacked into the city's propaganda network and replaced all the screens with cat videos."

Alice laughed, the memory bringing a smile to her face. "Oh my god, I thought Brayden was going to have an aneurysm when he saw that. His face turned so red, I thought he was going to explode."

As they continued to swap stories and reminisce about their adventures, Daniel couldn't help but feel a sense of pride and accomplishment. They had been through so much together, and somehow, they had managed to come out on top.

We may be a bunch of misfits and troublemakers, he thought, *but we've got each other's backs. And in a world as crazy as this one, that's all that really matters.*

Suddenly, a commotion erupted in the streets, drawing the group's attention. People were cheering and dancing, their faces alight with joy and disbelief. Daniel exchanged a puzzled glance with his friends before they made their way over to investigate.

As they approached, they noticed a large holographic screen displaying a news broadcast. The anchor, a woman with a shocked expression, announced, "In an unprecedented turn of events, the newly appointed government has declared a series of bizarre laws in the wake of Brayden Funkledor's removal."

The screen cut to a list of the new regulations, each more absurd than the last. "Effective immediately," the anchor continued, "all citizens are required to wear mismatched socks in public. Additionally, every Thursday has been designated as 'Opposite Day,' where citizens must speak and act in contradiction to their true intentions."

Daniel stared at the screen, his mouth agape. "Is this for real?" he muttered, turning to his friends.

Alice shrugged, a smirk playing on her lips. "I guess when you overthrow a tyrannical leader, anything goes."

Kyle, meanwhile, was already rummaging through his backpack. "I think I have an extra pair of mismatched socks in here somewhere," he said, his voice muffled by the bag's contents.

As the news report continued, the group couldn't help but laugh at the sheer ridiculousness of the situation. The anchor announced that a massive celebration was being planned in honor of their victory, complete with a parade featuring floats shaped like various office supplies.

"A stapler float?" Daniel snorted, shaking his head in disbelief. "I guess that's one way to stick it to Brayden."

Alice groaned at the pun, but a smile tugged at the corners of her mouth. "I can't believe this is our new reality," she said, gesturing to the chaos unfolding around them.

But maybe that's not such a bad thing, Daniel thought, watching as people embraced the absurdity with open arms. *In a world that's been so oppressive and bleak, a little bit of ridiculousness might be exactly what we need.*

As they stood there, surrounded by the laughter and joy of the liberated citizens, Daniel felt a sense of hope for the future. Sure, things were still a mess, and there was a lot of work to be done, but for the first time in a long time, he felt like anything was possible.

"Come on," he said, draping his arms around Alice and Kyle's shoulders. "Let's go find some mismatched socks and join the celebration. We've earned it."

With that, the trio set off into the streets, ready to embrace the chaos and absurdity of their brave new world.

As they wove their way through the crowded streets, Daniel couldn't help but marvel at the transformative power of laughter. The once-dreary city had come alive with a vibrant energy, the air filled with the sound of whoops and cheers as people reveled in their newfound freedom.

"Hey, look at that!" Kyle exclaimed, pointing to a group of people engaged in a spontaneous game of "pin the tie on the corporate drone."

Alice snorted, her eyes sparkling with mirth. "I never thought I'd see the day when office culture would become a source of entertainment."

Daniel grinned, feeling a sense of camaraderie with his fellow citizens. They had all endured so much under Brayden's oppressive rule, and now, they were finally free to let loose and embrace the absurdity of it all.

This is what we fought for, he thought, watching as a group of children ran by, their faces painted with bright colors and their laughter ringing through the air. *The right to be silly, to find joy in the little things, to not take ourselves so damn seriously all the time.*

As they approached the center of the celebration, Daniel spotted a makeshift stage where a band was setting up to play. The lead singer, a woman with a shock of purple hair and a mischievous grin, caught his eye and waved him over.

"Hey, hero!" she called out, her voice carrying over the din of the crowd. "Get your ass up here and join us for a song!"

Daniel hesitated, suddenly feeling self-conscious. But then he felt Alice's hand on his shoulder, giving him a reassuring squeeze.

"Go on," she urged, her eyes twinkling with encouragement. "Show them what you're made of."

With a deep breath and a nod, Daniel climbed onto the stage, grabbing the microphone as the band launched into a raucous rendition of "We're Not Gonna Take It." As he belted out the lyrics, he felt a rush of adrenaline coursing through his veins, the energy of the crowd lifting him up and carrying him away.

This is what it means to be alive, he thought, his voice soaring over the cheers and applause. *To stand up for what you believe in, to fight for a better world, and to never, ever stop laughing in the face of adversity.*

As the song came to a close, Daniel looked out over the sea of smiling faces, his heart swelling with pride and gratitude. They had done it. They had taken back their city, their lives, and their laughter. And nothing, not even the memory of Brayden's tyranny, could ever take that away from them again.

With a final whoop of joy, Daniel leaped off the stage and into the waiting arms of his friends, ready to embrace whatever ridiculous adventures the future might hold. Because in a world where anything was possible, laughter would always be their most powerful weapon.

Daniel, Alice, and Kyle burst through the doors of the Department of Redundancy Department, their laughter echoing off the sterile white walls.

"Can you believe," Kyle gasped between chuckles, "that we had to fill out Form 27B stroke 6...in triplicate?"

Alice snorted. "And then get it notarized by a one-armed notary!"

"Who then had to stamp it with the official Seal of Absurdity," Daniel added, wiping tears of mirth from his eyes. "I thought my hand was going to fall off from all that paperwork."

As they walked down the cracked sidewalk, still giggling, a robotic street cleaner veered erratically toward them, spraying sudsy water in wild arcs. Daniel nimbly sidestepped the deluge with a yelp. Alice wasn't so lucky.

"Gah, not again!" She frantically brushed at the spreading damp splotch on her shirt. "I swear these bots have it out for me."

"Maybe it's payback for you kicking that parking attendant bot last week," Kyle teased, deftly ducking under another spray of water.

Alice shot him a mock glare. "Hey, that was self-defense! The darn thing was going to give me a ticket for 'parking while sassy'."

Daniel chuckled and shook his head as he watched his friends bicker. Just another day in this crazy, messed up world of theirs. But somehow, with Kyle and Alice by his side, dodging malfunctioning robots and laughing in the face of bureaucratic insanity, it didn't seem so bad. Their shared mirth was a shield against the rampant absurdities that permeated every aspect of their lives under the rule of that nutjob Braydon Funkledor.

As they continued down the street, Daniel couldn't help but marvel at their ability to find humor in the midst of such dystopian madness. Maybe laughter really was the best medicine. Or maybe they were all just losing it. Either way, he was grateful to have friends who understood the importance of not taking life too seriously - even when the world seemed determined to crush your spirit under the weight of nonsensical regulations and defective machinery.

Alice skirted another errant spray from the cleaning bot, cursing colorfully. Kyle guffawed. Daniel allowed himself a small smile. Yep, just another wonderfully ridiculous day with his equally ludicrous pals in this funhouse mirror version of reality. He wouldn't have it any other way.

As they rounded the corner, Daniel spotted a familiar figure struggling with a large bag overflowing with mismatched socks. Mrs. Flibber, their eccentric neighbor, was muttering to herself as she tried to stuff yet another pair of clashing colors into the already bursting sack.

"Morning, Mrs. Flibber!" Daniel called out, trying to keep a straight face. "Doing some laundry?"

The elderly woman looked up, her face a mixture of exasperation and amusement. "Oh, hello, Daniel! No, no, not laundry. It's this darn new law, you know? Mismatched socks on Tuesdays! I swear, that Funkledor fellow must have a screw loose!"

Alice and Kyle exchanged a knowing glance, barely suppressing their laughter. Daniel, however, put on his most serious expression and nodded solemnly. "Ah, yes, the Sock Discordance Act of '35. A true cornerstone of our society."

Mrs. Flibber sighed heavily. "I just don't know how I'm going to keep up! I've got arthritis in my fingers, and sorting through all these socks is just too much!"

Daniel's eyes twinkled with mischief. "Well, Mrs. Flibber, have you considered wearing mismatched shoes instead? I mean, socks are hidden, but shoes? That's a real statement!"

The old woman's face lit up. "Oh, Daniel, you're a genius! Mismatched shoes! That'll show 'em!" She cackled with glee, dropping the sack of socks and hobbling back towards her house. "Thank you, dear!"

As Mrs. Flibber disappeared inside, the trio finally let loose, their laughter ringing through the street. "Mismatched shoes!" Kyle howled, clutching his sides. "Daniel, you're a mad genius!"

Alice wiped a tear from her eye, still giggling. "Poor Mrs. Flibber. But hey, at least she's got a plan now!"

Daniel grinned, feeling a warmth spread through his chest. These little moments of absurdity, shared with his best friends, made everything else bearable. "Come on, let's go meet up with Liz and Tim. I heard the café has a new policy on cup shapes that's causing quite the stir!"

The group set off, their laughter carrying them down the street and towards their next comedic adventure.

As they pushed open the door to the café, Daniel was immediately struck by the buzz of conversation filling the air. Patrons huddled around tables, gesticulating wildly as they debated what seemed to be the most pressing issue of the day: the merits of square versus round coffee cups.

"I'm telling you, squares are the way to go!" a bearded man exclaimed, slamming his fist on the table. "More stable, less spillage!"

His companion, a woman with bright purple hair, scoffed. "But round cups are classic! They're comfortable to hold, and they don't have those weird corners!"

Daniel exchanged an amused glance with Alice and Kyle as they wove their way through the passionate debates. Spotting Liz and Tim at a nearby table, they made their way over, dodging emphatic hand gestures and nearly colliding with a server carrying a tray of misshapen mugs.

"Hey, guys!" Liz greeted them, her eyes sparkling with mirth. "Can you believe this? People are actually arguing about cup shapes!"

Tim chuckled, shaking his head. "I mean, I guess it's better than debating the merits of Funkledor's latest decree. What was it again? Mandatory mime lessons for all citizens over 65?"

The group groaned in unison, collapsing into their seats. "Don't remind me," Alice said, burying her face in her hands. "I still have nightmares about my grandma's 'trapped in a box' routine."

As a server approached to take their order, Daniel couldn't help but notice the mix of square and round cups on their tray. He leaned in conspiratorially, a grin spreading across his face. "Hey, what do you think? Square or round?"

The server rolled their eyes, a smirk tugging at the corners of their mouth. "Honestly? I prefer triangles. Keeps things interesting."

The table erupted in laughter, drawing curious glances from the other patrons. Daniel sat back, basking in the warmth of his friends' company and the sheer ridiculousness of their world. If you couldn't laugh at the absurdity of it all, what was the point?

Alice leaned forward, a mischievous glint in her eye. "Okay, okay, but seriously, what was the most ridiculous executive order Funkledor ever issued? I vote for the mandatory 'Bring Your Pet to Work Day.'"

Kyle snorted, nearly choking on his coffee. "Oh, man, I remember that! My coworker brought his pet python. It escaped and caused a full-on panic in the office."

"That's nothing," Liz chimed in, her voice taking on a dramatic tone. "Remember when Funkledor declared that all citizens had to speak in rhyme on Thursdays? I got fined for 'insufficient whimsy' because I couldn't come up with a rhyme for 'orange.'"

The group burst into laughter, each taking turns imitating Funkledor's exaggerated hand gestures and nonsensical proclamations. Daniel puffed out his chest, putting on his best Funkledor impression. "By the power vested in me, I hereby declare that all citizens must wear their clothes inside out on alternate Tuesdays!"

The café filled with their laughter, drawing amused glances from the other patrons. A few even joined in, shouting out their own ridiculous Funkledor impressions.

As the laughter died down, Tim leaned in, a grin spreading across his face. "Speaking of ridiculous, did I ever tell you about the time I accidentally attended a Chuddie rally?"

The group shook their heads, their eyes wide with anticipation.

"Okay, so picture this," Tim began, his hands waving animatedly. "I was just walking down the street, minding my own business, when I saw this huge crowd gathered in the park. I thought, 'Hey, maybe it's a free concert or something,' so I decided to check it out."

He paused for dramatic effect, his eyes sparkling with mirth. "As I got closer, I realized everyone was wearing these bright yellow hats with little propellers on top. I mean, it was like a sea of spinning propellers!"

The group leaned in, hanging on his every word.

"So, I'm standing there, trying to figure out what's going on, when suddenly this guy jumps up on stage and starts shouting, 'Chud! Chud! Chud!' And the whole crowd just goes wild, spinning their propellers and chanting along with him."

Tim stood up, reenacting the scene with exaggerated gestures. He spun around, his arms flailing as he chanted, "Chud! Chud! Chud!"

The group erupted in laughter, their sides aching as they watched Tim's antics. He collapsed back into his seat, grinning from ear to ear.

"I had no idea what was happening, but I figured, 'When in Rome, right?' So, I started spinning my imaginary propeller and chanting along with everyone else. It wasn't until later that I found out it was a Chuddie rally!"

The friends wiped tears of laughter from their eyes, their cheeks flushed with mirth. In that moment, surrounded by the absurdity of their world and the warmth of their friendship, everything felt just a little bit brighter.

As the laughter subsided, Daniel found himself gazing out the café window, his thoughts drifting to the changes they had all experienced. The world outside was a kaleidoscope of absurdity, a constant reminder of the chaos that had become their new normal. He watched as a parade of people dressed as giant vegetables marched past, their costumes a riot of color against the gray cityscape.

"Hey, look at that," Daniel said, pointing out the window. "It's like a farmer's market on acid."

The others turned to look, their eyes widening at the surreal sight. A giant carrot walked arm in arm with an oversized tomato, while a massive head of lettuce bobbed along behind them. The parade-goers waved to the onlookers, their smiles visible through the mesh of their costumes.

Liz snorted. "I wonder what the occasion is. National Vegetable Day? Or maybe it's just another Tuesday in our crazy world."

Alice grinned. "I bet it's a protest against the new ban on imported produce. You know, the one where they claimed foreign fruits were a threat to national security?"

The group chuckled, shaking their heads at the absurdity of it all. In a world where nothing made sense, sometimes the only thing left to do was laugh.

As the parade disappeared around the corner, Liz reached for her mug, her eyes sparkling with mischief. She raised it high, the oversized ceramic dwarfing her hand.

"I'd like to propose a toast," she said, her voice ringing out through the café. "To us, for surviving this crazy world with our sanity mostly intact. And to the power of laughter, for getting us through even the darkest of times."

The others reached for their mugs, clinking them together with a resounding thud. Coffee sloshed over the sides, pooling on the table, but no one seemed to mind. They were too caught up in the moment, their faces split wide with grins.

"To us!" they chorused, their voices mingling with the sounds of the café.

As they sipped their coffee, Daniel felt a warmth spreading through his chest that had nothing to do with the hot liquid. It was the warmth of friendship, of knowing that no matter how crazy the world got, he would always have these people by his side.

And in that moment, surrounded by the laughter and love of his friends, Daniel knew that everything would be okay. They would face whatever challenges came their way, armed with humor and the unbreakable bonds of their friendship. And together, they would find a way to make even the most absurd of situations feel just a little bit brighter.

As they stepped out of the café, the group was immediately greeted by a street performer juggling flaming rubber chickens. The performer's face was painted in a garish array of colors, his movements exaggerated and comical as he tossed the blazing birds in a dizzying pattern.

"Well, that's something you don't see every day," Alice quipped, her eyebrows raised in amusement.

Daniel couldn't help but chuckle. "I don't know, in this city? I'd say flaming poultry is pretty par for the course."

The performer's antics quickly drew a crowd, and the friends found themselves swept up in the excitement. They clapped and cheered, their laughter mingling with the gasps and applause of the other onlookers.

As the performer took his final bow, the chickens extinguished and tucked safely under his arms, Kyle turned to the others with a grin. "You know, I think I'm starting to appreciate the absurdity of this place. It keeps things interesting, at least."

Liz nodded in agreement. "Definitely beats the monotony of a normal, well-functioning society."

They continued their walk through the city, the streets a kaleidoscope of color and chaos. Every building was adorned with vibrant, nonsensical murals, each one more surreal than the last.

"Is that... Brayden Funkledor riding a unicycle on the moon?" Tim asked, pointing to a particularly bizarre painting.

Daniel squinted at the mural, his head tilted to the side. "I think it is. And... is he juggling planets?"

"Of course he is," Alice said with a snort. "I mean, why wouldn't the supreme leader of our dystopian society be a cosmic unicyclist?"

The group paused to admire the mural, their eyes tracing the brushstrokes that brought the absurd scene to life. In a world where nothing made sense, there was something strangely comforting about the chaotic creativity that surrounded them.

"You know," Daniel mused, "I never thought I'd say this, but I'm starting to appreciate the beauty in the madness. It's like the city itself is a work of art, just waiting to be explored."

Liz draped an arm around his shoulders, pulling him close. "That's the spirit, Daniel. Embrace the chaos, and the chaos will embrace you."

They stood there for a moment longer, letting the vibrant hues of the mural wash over them. And as they did, Daniel felt a sense of peace settle in his chest. The world might be a crazy, nonsensical place, but with his friends by his side, he knew that he could find joy and wonder in even the most absurd of circumstances.

As they continued their leisurely stroll through the city streets, a boisterous voice cut through the air. "Authentic alien souvenirs! Get your genuine extraterrestrial memorabilia here!"

Daniel's eyes widened as he spotted a street vendor hawking his wares from a rickety wooden cart. The man was dressed in a silver jumpsuit, complete with a tinfoil hat that glinted in the sunlight. Displayed on the cart were an array of bizarre items, from glowing green rocks to pulsating purple orbs.

"Well, well, well," Daniel said, rubbing his hands together. "What have we here?"

He sauntered over to the cart, his friends trailing behind him with amused expressions. The vendor flashed a toothy grin, holding up a glow-in-the-dark alien hat. "Ah, my friend! You look like a man who appreciates the finer things in life. This hat was worn by the leader of the Zorgon invasion fleet himself!"

Daniel raised an eyebrow, barely suppressing a smirk. "Is that so? And how much for this piece of intergalactic history?"

The vendor leaned in conspiratorially. "For you, my friend? A mere fifty credits."

"Fifty credits?" Daniel scoffed. "For a hat that looks like it was made in a basement? I'll give you twenty."

The haggling continued back and forth, with Daniel's friends chiming in with their own outrageous offers. Finally, the vendor relented, throwing in a free "I Survived the Invasion" sticker to sweeten the deal.

As they walked away, Daniel proudly donned his new hat, the alien's eyes glowing an eerie green. "I can't believe I just paid thirty credits for this thing," he said with a laugh.

"Hey, at least you got a sticker," Kyle said, slapping the adhesive onto his jacket. "Now everyone will know how brave we were during the fake invasion."

Their laughter echoed through the streets as they continued their journey, the absurdity of their purchases only adding to the hilarity of the moment.

As they approached their neighborhood, Kyle's eyes lit up with mischief. "Hey, guys," he said, lowering his voice to a conspiratorial whisper. "Want to play a quick game of 'Dodge the Drone'?"

Alice groaned, but there was a glint of excitement in her eyes. "Kyle, you know that's illegal, right?"

"Only if you get caught," he said with a wink. "Come on, it'll be fun!"

Daniel hesitated for a moment, weighing the risks against the thrill of the game. But as he looked around at his friends' eager faces, he felt a surge of reckless abandon. "Ah, what the hell," he said, grinning. "Let's do it."

The group quickly scanned the skies, spotting a surveillance drone hovering nearby. With a nod from Kyle, they scattered, ducking behind dumpsters and darting into alleyways.

Daniel's heart raced as he pressed himself against a brick wall, watching the drone's blinking lights draw closer. He held his breath, waiting for the perfect moment to make his move.

Just as the drone was about to pass overhead, he sprinted across the street, his friends hot on his heels. They wove through the maze of buildings, their laughter echoing off the concrete as they dodged and weaved, the drone always just a step behind.

For a moment, Daniel forgot about the absurdity of their world, forgot about the constant surveillance and the nonsensical laws. All that mattered was the rush of adrenaline, the feeling of his muscles straining as he pushed himself to the limit.

And as they finally tumbled into the safety of Daniel's apartment building, breathless and giddy with excitement, he couldn't help but feel a sense of triumph. They might live in a world gone mad, but together, they could find joy and adventure in even the darkest of times.

As the door to Daniel's apartment swung open, the group stumbled inside, their laughter filling the air. Daniel collapsed onto the couch, his glow-in-the-dark alien hat slightly askew, while Kyle and Liz sprawled across the armchairs. Alice perched herself on the arm of the sofa, her eyes sparkling with mirth.

"Did you see the look on that drone's face when we gave it the slip?" Kyle chuckled, wiping a tear from his eye. "I swear, it looked like it was about to short-circuit!"

"Drones don't have faces, you idiot," Liz retorted, tossing a throw pillow at him. "But I have to admit, that was pretty epic."

Daniel grinned, his chest still heaving from the exertion. "I can't believe we actually pulled that off. I thought for sure we were going to get caught."

"Nah," Alice said, waving a hand dismissively. "We're too quick for those clunky old drones. Besides, what's the worst they could do? Make us wear mismatched socks for a week?"

The group erupted into another fit of laughter, their exhaustion giving way to a sense of camaraderie and resilience. They had faced the absurdity of their world head-on and come out on top, their spirits unbroken.

As the laughter died down, Alice's eyes suddenly lit up with excitement. "Hey, you know what we should do next? We should take a road trip to see the World's Largest Ball of Yarn!"

Daniel raised an eyebrow, his curiosity piqued. "The World's Largest Ball of Yarn? Where's that?"

"It's in some tiny town called Flibbertigibbet," Alice replied, her grin widening. "Apparently, it's made up of over a million feet of yarn and weighs like five tons or something."

Kyle snorted. "Only in this crazy world would something like that exist. I'm in."

Liz nodded, her eyes twinkling with mischief. "Me too. I've always wanted to see a ball of yarn bigger than my apartment."

Daniel leaned back, his mind already racing with possibilities. "You know what? Let's do it. Let's take a road trip to see the World's Largest Ball of Yarn. Because why the hell not?"

The group cheered, their enthusiasm infectious. In a world where nothing made sense, where bureaucracy and absurdity reigned supreme, they had found a way to embrace the chaos and find joy in the unexpected.

And as they began to plan their next adventure, Daniel couldn't help but feel a sense of gratitude for his friends, for their unwavering spirit and their ability to find humor in even the darkest of times. Together, they could face anything this crazy world threw at them, one ridiculous adventure at a time.

The neon sign on Joe's Diner flickered and buzzed, casting an eerie glow on the cracked vinyl booth where Daniel, Alice, and Kyle slouched, grinning like idiots. A tattered menu lay before them.

"I'll have the Brayden Burger with a side of Chuddie Fries," Daniel snorted, slapping the laminated menu. "And a tall glass of Kool-Aid to wash it down."

Alice cackled and pretended to choke. "Oh god, spare me! I've had enough Kool-Aid for a lifetime after that Chuddie cult fiasco."

Kyle shook his head, smirking. "Never thought I'd miss the days when this dump just served up greasy slop on a plate. Now it's greasy slop with a dystopian twist."

"Hey, at least we made it through," Daniel said, his laughter fading into a wistful smile. "All that chaos, the insanity...and here we are. Together."

Alice reached across the table and squeezed his hand. "Amen to that. We're the Three Musketeers of the apocalypse."

Kyle raised an imaginary glass. "All for one and one for all, bitches!"

Their laughter echoed through the empty diner as they clinked invisible glasses.

Daniel's mind wandered to the surreal journey they'd been on - the mad scramble for truth in a world gone batshit crazy. It felt good to just sit here and revel in the absurdity of it all with his best friends by his side.

The trio stepped out of Joe's Diner and onto the cracked sidewalk, blinking in the harsh sunlight. The city sprawled before them, a bizarre patchwork of boarded-up storefronts and garishly colored billboards spouting off slogans like "Ignorance is Bliss" and "Conform and Be Happy."

As they walked, they passed a street performer dressed head to toe in a tattered Brayden costume, complete with a crudely fashioned papier-mâché mask. He juggled crumpled newspapers with sensational headlines like "Scientists Confirm: Earth is Flat" and "Lizard People Control Government, Says Inside Source."

A small crowd had gathered to watch, chuckling and tossing coins into the performer's upturned hat.

"Jesus, is this what passes for entertainment now?" Kyle scoffed, shaking his head.

"Hey, you gotta admire the guy's commitment to the bit," Alice said with a smirk. "Brayden always did know how to work a crowd."

Daniel couldn't help but laugh. In a world where the line between truth and fiction had been so thoroughly erased, there was something perversely comical about seeing Brayden's likeness literally juggling fake news.

It was a stark reminder of just how much had changed, and yet, how little had really been resolved. The absurdity that had nearly destroyed them all still lurked around every corner.

But as he glanced at Alice and Kyle, their eyes bright with mirth even in the face of such madness, Daniel felt a swell of hope. Together, they would find a way to navigate this brave new world - one laugh at a time.

As they continued their stroll, Alice suddenly stopped dead in her tracks, her eyes widening as she pointed at a massive billboard looming overhead. "Holy shit, guys. Get a load of this."

Daniel and Kyle followed her gaze, their jaws dropping in unison. The billboard featured a garish montage of explosions, screaming contestants, and a bold, red title that read: "Survivor: Dumbocracy - Only the Most Gullible Will Prevail!"

"You've got to be kidding me," Daniel muttered, running a hand through his hair. "They're actually turning this whole mess into a reality show?"

"I guess it was only a matter of time," Kyle said with a snort. "I mean, what's more entertaining than watching a bunch of idiots stumble their way through a post-truth apocalypse?"

Alice let out a bark of laughter. "I can see it now: challenges like 'Who Can Spread the Most Misinformation in 24 Hours' and 'Conspiracy Theory Scavenger Hunt.'"

"Don't forget the immunity idols," Daniel chimed in, grinning despite himself. "Instead of hidden statues, they'll be fake news articles. Find the most viral one, and you're safe from elimination."

They dissolved into a fit of giggles, their mirth echoing off the crumbling buildings. It was a testament to how far they'd come, Daniel mused, that they could find humor in even the most distressing reminders of their reality.

Still chuckling, they made their way to the local park, where they'd agreed to meet up with Liz and Tim. As they approached the designated spot, Daniel spotted the couple sitting on a bench, hunched over a laptop and speaking animatedly into a microphone.

"...and that, dear listeners, is why the government is definitely not putting mind-control chemicals in our water supply," Liz was saying, her voice dripping with sarcasm. "I mean, come on. If they were, wouldn't we all be a lot more obedient by now?"

Tim let out an exaggerated sigh. "Guess we'll have to find another explanation for why people keep believing this bullshit."

Daniel couldn't help but smile as he and the others drew near. "Hard at work debunking the latest conspiracy theories, I see."

Liz looked up, her face breaking into a grin. "Someone's got to do it. You wouldn't believe the kind of crap people are coming up with these days."

"Oh, I think we've got a pretty good idea," Alice said, plopping down on the bench beside her. "We just saw a billboard for 'Survivor: Dumbocracy.'"

Tim let out a low whistle. "Damn. And here I thought we'd hit rock bottom with the Flat Earth revival movement."

"Never underestimate the depths of human stupidity," Kyle said sagely, taking a seat on the grass. "So, what's new in the world of truth-seeking podcasters?"

As Liz and Tim launched into a recap of their latest adventures in debunking, Daniel felt a warmth bloom in his chest. It was moments like these - surrounded by friends who refused to surrender to the absurdity, who fought back with laughter and relentless pursuit of the truth - that gave him the strength to keep going.

They might be living in a world gone mad, but together, they would find a way to make sense of it all. One ridiculous conspiracy theory at a time.

In a dimly lit, comically secretive lab, the rogue scientists huddled around their microscopes, squinting at the bizarre human behavior charts that more closely resembled abstract art than scientific data. Dr. Olivia Neumann, her hair haphazardly tied back and a look of intense concentration on her face, leaned closer to the eyepiece, muttering under her breath.

"Fascinating," she said, her voice a mix of awe and disbelief. "These patterns of irrationality are unlike anything I've ever seen."

Her colleague, Dr. Ethan Rosenberg, glanced up from his own microscope, a wry smile playing on his lips. "It's like they've elevated absurdity to an art form."

"But how do we combat it?" Dr. Neumann wondered aloud, straightening up and stretching her back. "We can't just sit back and watch as the world descends into utter chaos."

Dr. Rosenberg tapped his chin thoughtfully, his eyes sparkling with a hint of mischief. "What if we fight fire with fire? Use the very tools of absurdity against them?"

"What do you mean?" Dr. Neumann asked, quirking an eyebrow.

"Holograms," Dr. Rosenberg said, a grin spreading across his face. "We create our own absurd holograms to counter the nonsense. Fight irrationality with even greater irrationality."

Dr. Neumann stared at him for a moment, then burst out laughing. "You're mad," she said, shaking her head. "But it just might work."

As the scientists debated the merits of their unorthodox plan, their laughter echoing off the lab's walls, Daniel and his friends gathered around a makeshift stage in the park. Professor Zander, his wild grey hair sticking out at odd angles, strode onto the stage, a rubber chicken in one hand and a pair of oversized glasses perched precariously on his nose.

"Ladies and gentlemen!" he bellowed, his voice carrying across the park. "Welcome to today's lecture on the importance of critical thinking!"

The crowd, a mix of amused and bewildered faces, settled in as Professor Zander launched into his hilariously convoluted speech. He waved the rubber chicken for emphasis, eliciting chuckles from the audience, and donned the oversized glasses to peer at them with exaggerated scrutiny.

"In a world where truth is stranger than fiction," he declared, "it is our duty, nay, our sacred obligation, to question everything!"

Daniel leaned over to Alice, grinning. "He's really embracing the absurdity, isn't he?"

Alice smirked, nodding. "If you can't beat 'em, join 'em."

As Professor Zander continued his lecture, peppering his words with increasingly ridiculous anecdotes and props, Daniel felt a sense of pride swell within him. This was what they were fighting for - the freedom to think, to question, to find humor in even the darkest of times.

And with friends like these by his side, he knew they could face whatever challenges this bizarre new world threw their way, one preposterous conspiracy theory at a time.

Kyle stood in line at the coffee shop, his patience wearing thinner by the second. All he wanted was a simple cup of coffee, but the new bureaucratic system seemed determined to make it as difficult as possible.

"Next!" the barista called out, a bored expression on her face.

Kyle stepped forward, mustering a smile. "Hi, I'd like a medium coffee, please."

The barista stared at him blankly. "I'm sorry, sir, but you'll need to fill out Form C-137 before placing your order."

"Form C-137?" Kyle asked, his eye twitching. "What the hell is that?"

"It's a requisition form for caffeine-based beverages," she explained, sliding a comically long piece of paper across the counter. "Please answer all questions in triplicate and provide a DNA sample for verification purposes."

Kyle glanced down at the form, his exasperation growing with each absurd question. "'Have you ever dreamed of being a turnip?' What does that have to do with ordering coffee?"

Daniel and Alice, standing behind him in line, couldn't contain their laughter. "Looks like the Chuddie influence is still going strong," Alice quipped.

Kyle shot them a withering glare before turning back to the barista. "Look, I just want a coffee. Can't we skip all this nonsense?"

The barista shrugged apologetically. "I'm sorry, sir, but rules are rules. If you don't complete the form, I'm afraid I can't serve you."

With an exaggerated sigh, Kyle snatched the form and began scribbling furiously, his frustration evident in every stroke of the pen. Daniel and Alice, meanwhile, could barely contain their mirth, their laughter echoing through the coffee shop.

As they finally exited the shop, Kyle clutching his hard-earned coffee like a trophy, Daniel found himself reflecting on their journey. The absurdity they'd faced, the challenges they'd overcome - it had all brought them closer together, forging an unbreakable bond of friendship and resilience.

"You know," he mused, "as ridiculous as this all is, I wouldn't trade it for anything. We've been through so much together, and it's only made us stronger."

Alice nodded, a smile playing at the corners of her mouth. "Who knew the key to surviving a dystopian nightmare would be a healthy dose of humor and sarcasm?"

Their laughter was suddenly interrupted by the sound of music blaring from the park across the street. A group of enthusiastic Chuddie converts had apparently decided to throw an impromptu dance party, their flailing limbs and off-key singing drawing curious glances from passersby.

"Oh my god," Kyle groaned, taking a sip of his coffee. "Just when you think things can't get any weirder."

But Daniel was already moving towards the park, a grin spreading across his face. "Come on, guys. If you can't beat 'em, join 'em!"

And with that, the trio found themselves swept up in the chaos, their laughter mingling with the pulsing beat of the music as they danced alongside the Chuddie converts, embracing the absurdity of the moment with open arms.

Alice broke away from the group, still chuckling at the impromptu dance party, and made her way towards a small stand set up near the edge of the park. A sign hung above it, proudly proclaiming "Truth Bombs: Explosively Honest Candies!"

As she approached, Alice recognized the vendor as a former Chuddie, his once-pristine uniform now adorned with an array of colorful patches and pins. He grinned at her, holding out a basket filled with small, individually wrapped candies.

"Well, well, if it isn't the famous Alice," he said, his eyes twinkling with mirth. "Care to try a Truth Bomb? Guaranteed to blow your mind with wit and wisdom!"

Alice smirked, plucking a candy from the basket. "I don't know, my mind's been blown enough lately. But I suppose one more explosion couldn't hurt."

She unwrapped the candy, popping it into her mouth and letting the sweet, tangy flavor burst across her tongue. As she chewed, she unfolded the tiny slip of paper that had been wrapped around the candy.

"'The only thing more absurd than the lies we're told is the truth we refuse to believe,'" she read aloud, raising an eyebrow. "Damn, that's actually pretty deep."

The vendor chuckled, leaning forward conspiratorially. "Between you and me, I think people are finally starting to wake up to the bullshit. Your little group's made quite an impact around here."

Alice felt a swell of pride in her chest. They had fought so hard to expose the truth, to break through the fog of lies and manipulation that had consumed their society for so long. And now, here was proof that their efforts hadn't been in vain.

She bought a handful of Truth Bombs, tucking them into her pocket with a grin. "Keep fighting the good fight," she told the vendor, who saluted her with a wink.

As Alice rejoined her friends, Daniel waved her over to a large canvas set up in the middle of the park. A crowd had gathered around it, watching as a group of artists worked to paint a sprawling mural.

"Check it out," Daniel said, pointing to the colorful scene taking shape before them. "It's us!"

Sure enough, the mural depicted their ragtag group in all their glory, from Daniel's determined stance to Kyle's exasperated eye rolls. Brayden and the rogue scientists made appearances as well, their caricatured faces twisted into comical expressions of frustration and defeat.

But what struck Alice most was the sense of hope that emanated from the mural. Despite the chaos and absurdity that surrounded them, the artists had captured the unbreakable spirit of their little rebellion, the unwavering belief that truth and reason would ultimately prevail.

As they watched, more and more people began to join in, adding their own brushstrokes and flourishes to the mural. It was a testament to the power of their message, the way it had resonated with so many others who had grown tired of the lies and manipulation.

Alice felt a hand on her shoulder and turned to see Kyle standing beside her, a rare smile on his face. "You know, for a bunch of misfits and troublemakers, we make a pretty good team," he said, his voice uncharacteristically soft.

She leaned into him, feeling the warmth of his presence and the strength of their bond. "Yeah," she agreed, her own smile spreading across her face. "I guess we do."

And as the sun began to set over the park, casting a golden glow across the mural and the laughing, paint-splattered crowd, Alice knew that no matter what absurdities the future might hold, they would face them together - with humor, with heart, and with an unshakable commitment to the truth.

As the group admired their handiwork, a sudden commotion erupted nearby. Tim, who had been fiddling with a mysterious device he'd found in the park, accidentally triggered a holographic projection of Brayden's infamous speeches. The larger-than-life image of Brayden, with his signature smirk and ridiculous hairdo, loomed over the startled crowd.

"My fellow Chuddies!" the hologram boomed, its voice echoing through the park. "Believe me when I say that the truth is whatever we want it to be!"

For a moment, panic rippled through the gathered people, their laughter turning to gasps of horror. But then, as the absurdity of the situation sank in, the gasps transformed into roars of laughter. Daniel, Alice, Kyle, and the others clutched their sides, tears streaming down their faces as they watched the holographic Brayden spout his nonsensical rhetoric.

"Wow, Tim," Daniel managed between guffaws, "you really know how to bring back the memories!"

Tim, looking sheepish but amused, shrugged his shoulders. "What can I say? Old habits die hard."

As the hologram fizzled out, the group made their way to a nearby park bench, still chuckling at the unexpected blast from the past. They settled onto the bench, shoulder to shoulder, as the sun began its slow descent towards the horizon.

"You know," Alice mused, her eyes fixed on the vibrant oranges and pinks of the sunset, "I never thought I'd say this, but I'm actually excited to see what tomorrow brings."

Kyle raised an eyebrow, a smirk playing at the corner of his mouth. "Even if it means more holographic Braydens popping up when we least expect it?"

Alice laughed, playfully swatting at his arm. "Especially then! I mean, how else are we going to keep our wits sharp and our humor intact?"

Daniel leaned back, his arms stretched along the back of the bench. "I don't know about you guys, but I'm thinking of starting a Brayden impersonation contest. You know, to keep his memory alive."

The group erupted into another round of laughter, their voices carrying through the park as the last rays of sunlight danced across their faces. They traded jokes and ideas, each more outlandish than the last, as they envisioned a future filled with laughter, camaraderie, and the occasional absurdity.

As the stars began to wink into existence above them, Alice felt a sense of contentment settle over her. Sure, their world was still a crazy, mixed-up place, but with her friends by her side and a never-ending supply of humor to keep them going, she knew they could face anything.

"Here's to the future," she said, raising an imaginary glass in a toast. "May it be filled with truth, laughter, and the occasional holographic Brayden to keep us on our toes."

The others raised their own imaginary glasses, their smiles wide and their hearts light. "To the future," they echoed, their voices ringing out into the night sky, a promise of hope and hilarity in the face of whatever challenges lay ahead.

Just as their laughter began to fade, a majestic bald eagle soared overhead, its wings spread wide against the darkening sky. The group watched in awe as the bird circled above them, its piercing gaze seeming to lock onto their little gathering.

"Well, if that isn't a sign from the universe, I don't know what is," Kyle quipped, his eyes following the eagle's path.

Suddenly, the eagle released a single feather from its plumage, the delicate object spiraling down towards them. It landed softly on Daniel's lap, and he picked it up gingerly, holding it between his fingers like a precious artifact.

"Looks like the universe has a sense of humor, too," he said, a grin spreading across his face. "I mean, what are the odds of a bald eagle dropping a feather on us right now?"

Alice reached out to touch the feather, her fingers brushing against its soft edges. "Maybe it's a reminder," she mused, her voice taking on a more serious tone. "A reminder of everything we've been through, and everything we've learned."

Liz nodded, her eyes shining with a mix of emotion and mirth. "We've come a long way, haven't we? From being lost in a sea of fake news and conspiracies to finding our way back to the truth, and to each other."

Tim draped an arm around Liz's shoulders, pulling her close. "And we couldn't have done it without a healthy dose of laughter along the way. I mean, can you imagine facing all of this without being able to find the humor in it?"

The group murmured their agreement, each lost in their own thoughts for a moment. Daniel twirled the feather between his fingers, a small smile playing at the corners of his mouth.

"You know what this means, right?" he said, his eyes twinkling with mischief. "We're officially the chosen ones. The universe has spoken, and it's our destiny to keep fighting the good fight, one absurd challenge at a time."

Kyle let out a snort of laughter, shaking his head. "I don't know about you, but I'm ready for whatever this crazy world throws at us next. Bring on the Brayden holograms, the Chuddie Fries, and the Dumbocracy survivors. We've got this."

As the group erupted into another fit of laughter, the eagle let out a piercing cry from above, as if in agreement. They looked up to see the bird soaring off into the distance, its silhouette growing smaller against the backdrop of the stars.

And with that, they knew that no matter what hilarity lay ahead, they would face it together, armed with the power of friendship, laughter, and the occasional cosmic sign from a meddling bald eagle.

The End.

Don't miss out!

Visit the website below and you can sign up to receive emails whenever Aaron Abilene publishes a new book. There's no charge and no obligation.

https://books2read.com/r/B-A-YOIP-QXKGF

BOOKS 2 READ

Connecting independent readers to independent writers.

Also by Aaron Abilene

505
505
505: Resurrection

Balls
Dead Awake
Before The Dead Awake
Dead Sleep
Bulletproof Balls

Carnival Game
Full Moon Howl
Donovan
Shades of Z

Codename
The Man in The Mini Van

Deadeye
Deadeye & Friends
Cowboys Vs Aliens

Ferris
Life in Prescott
Afterlife in Love
Tragic Heart

Island
Paradise Island
The Lost Island
The Lost Island 2
The Lost Island 3
The Island 2

Pandemic
Pandemic

Prototype
Prototype
The Compound

Slacker
Slacker 2
Slacker 3
Slacker: Dead Man Walkin'

Survivor Files
Survivor Files: Day 1
Survivor Files : Day 1 Part 2
Survivor Files : Day 2
Survivor Files : On The Run
Survivor Files : Day 3
Survivor Files : Day 4
Survivor Files : Day 5
Survivor Files : Day 6
Survivor Files : Day 7
Survivor Files : Day 8
Survivor Files : Day 9
Survivor Files : Day 10
Survivor Files : Day 11
Survivor Files : Day 12
Survivor Files : Day 13
Survivor Files : Day 14
Survivor Files : Day 15
Survivor Files : Day 16
Survivor Files : Day 17
Survivor Files : Day 18

Texas

Devil Child of Texas
A Vampire in Texas

The Author
Breaking Wind
Yellow Snow
Dragon Snatch
Golden Showers
Nether Region
Evil Empire

Thomas
Quarantine
Contagion
Eradication
Isolation
Immune
Pathogen
Bloodline
Decontaminated

TPD
Trailer Park Diaries
Trailer Park Diaries 2
Trailer Park Diaries 3

Virus
Raising Hell

Zombie Bride
Zombie Bride
Zombie Bride 2
Zombie Bride 3

Standalone
The Victims of Pinocchio
A Christmas Nightmare
Pain
Fat Jesus
A Zombie's Revenge
The Headhunter
Crash
Tranq
The Island
Dog
The Quiet Man
Joe Superhero
Feral
Good Guys
Romeo and Juliet and Zombies
The Gamer
Becoming Alpha
Dead West
Small Town Blues

Shades of Z: Redux
The Gift of Death
Killer Claus
Skarred
Home Sweet Home
Alligator Allan
10 Days
Army of The Dumbest Dead
Kid
The Cult of Stupid
9 Time Felon
Slater
Bad Review: Hannah Dies
Me Again
Maurice and Me
The Family Business
Lightning Rider : Better Days
Lazy Boyz
The Sheep
Wild
The Flood
Extinction
Good Intentions
Dark Magic
Sparkles The Vampire Clown
From The Future, Stuck in The Past
Rescue
Knock Knock
Creep
Honest John
Urbex
She's Psycho
Unfinished

Neighbors
Misery, Nevada
Vicious Cycle
Relive
Romeo and Juliet: True Love Conquers All
Dead Road
Florida Man
Hunting Sarah
The Great American Zombie Novel
Carnage
Marge 3 Toes
Random Acts of Stupidity
Born Killer
The Abducted
Whiteboy
Broken Man
Graham Hiney
Bridge
15
Paper Soldiers
Zartan
The Concepts of a Plan
The Firsts in Life
Giant Baby

Milton Keynes UK
Ingram Content Group UK Ltd.
UKHW030912121124
451094UK00001B/109

9 798227 276100